國貿
船務英文

許坤金 / 著

五南圖書出版公司 印行

推薦序

　　本人與作者早年共事於怡和集團的船務部，我比他晚進公司三年，在業務方面常受到作者的指導，由於許坤金先生待人誠懇熱心，處事積極樂觀，因此當年有很多貨主都與他關係很好，怡和的長官及船東也非常倚重他。

　　後來本人赴美改行做貿易，數年後回到臺灣，加入亞慶貿易公司，得知許坤金先生已榮膺祥天船務代理公司總經理一職，其實我對這個消息一點也不覺得意外，認識他的貨主及船務界朋友，也咸認怡和集團慧眼識英雄，拔擢一位學識、經驗、英日文俱佳的人來擔當要職，領導其關係企業，可謂適得其所。

　　民國八十四年，許坤金先生成立跨世紀企業管理顧問公司，十六年來他舉辦的「船務實務」企業講座，參加者眾，甚獲好評，幾已成為進出口廠商船務人員的進修搖籃。由於本人畢業於臺灣師範大學英文系，又曾擔任教職，曾經受邀旁聽許坤金先生主講的「船務英文」課程，發現他的教學內容紮實，實務舉例生動有趣，尤其他那深入淺出的解說功力，能得到程度參差不齊的學員的一致稱許，實在難得。現在他願以其在業界多年的經驗及專業知識，著手整理出書，嘉惠貿易界朋友，這種經驗傳承的精神，委實值得學習及肯定。

　　本人深感此書極具參考價值，故樂於大力推薦並為之作序。

亞慶貿易有限公司

前總經理　楊卓融

自 序

　　船務雖然是國際貿易中最後的一項工作，但攸關公司對客戶履行交貨的成敗，船務人員從公司接到訂單開始，就要擬訂裝船日期、預估箱數及材數、計算運費、催促工廠按時交貨、預訂艙位、準備報關及辦理押匯事宜等，在這過程中，還需要跟 Buyer 連絡有關的事情，比如說信用狀的交貨期、有效期、運輸、保險等條款的內容，如有不妥時，要求修改 L/C，或為因應客戶對裝船 Delay、貨品數量不符、Item 搞錯等 Complaint 的回函。由此可知外銷人員要能獨立作業，從接單到出貨完成，除了實務經驗之外，也需要專業的英文來處理相關的種種問題。坊間國貿英文的書籍很多，但涉及船務的部分少之又少，幾乎沒有一套專門針對船務方面的英文書籍。

　　有鑒於此，作者以在貿易及船務界工作多年的經驗，針對貿易船務的工作上，實際可能遭遇的問題，提供應對的英文寫作技巧，配合深入淺出的文法說明，讓讀者能在很短的時間內，學到既完整又專業的船務英文，進而在處理 Shipping 的工作上更順手、更有效率，這是作者當初下筆的心願及期望。

　　作者才疏學淺，本書如有遺漏、錯誤之處，尚祈各界先進不吝指正。

許坤金　謹識

2022 年 12 月

作者許坤金與台塑關係企業董事長王永慶先生合影

作者應經濟部外銷服務團邀請在臺北國貿局大禮堂演講

臺北市海運承攬運送業公會邀請作者專題演講

作者於外貿協會國際企業人才培訓中心擔任講師

目　錄

Unit

1

催促 Buyer 速開 L/C

🔒 說　明

　　一般來說廠商接到國外 Buyer 開來的訂單，除非是很熟的客戶，否則不敢貿然發單下去生產，因爲怕做了以後，客戶的信用狀或貨款沒有寄來，那生產好的東西，豈不變成存貨，鑑於過去二、三十年來，臺灣不少廠商因爲這樣而蒙受損失，因此我們最好還是等收到 L/C 或部分貨款後，再開始生產會比較穩當。但要催促 Buyer 早日開立 L/C，一定要有很好的理由來說服他，在這裡我們列舉四種。

第一種理由

In order to book the shipping space at an earlier date.
爲了要早一天預訂艙位。

■ 範　例

　　The purchase order stipulates shipment to be effected during July and L/C should reach us by the end of June. However as of this date, it appears that we have not received your L/C. In order to book the shipping space at an earlier date, you are requested to have the L/C opened immediately.

We appreciate your immediate attention to this matter.

翻譯

採購訂單規定要在七月間出貨，而且信用狀要在六月底前到達我們手上，但到目前為止，我們似乎還沒有接到您的信用狀，為了便於早一天去預訂艙位，我們請求您馬上開立信用狀。

我們很感激您對此事的立即關心。

解說

1. Stipulate：（規定）及物動詞，指合約或法律條款的規定，其名詞為 Stipulation（合約或法律的條款）。

2. Shipment to be effected 或 Shipment to be made：這是 Effect shipment、Make shipment 的被動語態，均為（裝運、出貨）的意思。

嚴格地說，Make shipment（裝運、出貨）與 Make delivery（交貨）是有差別的，但由於國際貿易中的交貨條件 FOB、CFR 及 CIF 均以出口港貨物裝載於船上（Loaded on board），視為賣方已交貨，因此 Make shipment 就等於 Make delivery。訂單中或 L/C 中的 Date of shipment，也等於 Date of delivery，但在進口商提貨時最好用 Take delivery（提貨），不要用 Take shipment。

3. L/C should reach us：也可以改成 L/C should arrive，但要注意的是 Reach 是及物動詞，後面一定要加受詞 us，而 Arrive 是不及物動詞，後面就不要再加受詞 us 了。

> **補充說明**
>
> Arrive 後面如果要接地方的名詞時，Arrive 後面一定要先加上一介系詞，再加地方的名詞。如 Arrive in Taipei（到達臺北）、Arrive at station（到達車站），大地方用 in，小地方用 at，但如果是指船抵達某港口時，不論其港口大小一律用 at，例如：The ship arrives at New York.；The ship arrives at Keelung.

4. As of this date：（到今天為止）= So far（到目前為止），使用這個片語 As of this date，請注意 Date 不是 Day，Date 是指某月某日的日期，而 Day 是指時間、日子而言。因此如有問句 What's the date today? 正確的回答是 Today is <u>April 15, 2022</u>（或其他日期），不能回答 Today is <u>Monday</u>（或其他星期幾），因為不論星期幾，都是屬於日子、時間而言。有了這個正確的觀念，您就不會把 L/C expiry date（信用狀到期日）寫成 L/C expiry day 或把 Shipping date 寫成 Shipping day。

5. To book the shipping space at an earlier date：（早一天預訂艙位）。

　5-1. 我們一般常說去船公司簽 Space，英文就是 Book the shipping space。

　5-2. At an earlier date（早一天或早一點的日期），而 At an <u>early</u> date 則是日內、近日的意思，兩者不太一樣請注意。

6. It appears that we have not received your L/C.：（我們似乎還沒有接到您的信用狀。）此句也可寫成：We have not received your L/C.（我們還沒有接到您的信用狀。）但前句使用 It appears，顯得比較客氣而有禮貌。

　　It appears = It seems（似乎）這件事情看起來……

　　例如：It seems that he is ill.（他似乎病了。）

7. You are requested to have the L/C opened immediately.：

7-1. 此處用被動語態 You are requested...（您被要求立刻開立信用狀。）比用主動語態 We request you...（我們要求您……），聽起來比較客氣。

7-2. 另外，To have the L/C opened（開立信用狀），也可以用 To open the L/C 代替，但使用前者，文辭比較優雅，其句型結構分析如下：

　　在英文裡，請人家或叫人家替您做事情的動詞，一般常用的只有四個：Have、Make、Let 及 Get，翻譯成使、叫、讓皆可。舉例來說：

　　I had Peter to fix my car.（我叫 Peter 修理我的車子。）

　　I made Peter to fix my car.（我叫 Peter 修理我的車子。）

　　I let Peter to fix my car.（我叫 Peter 修理我的車子。）

　　I got Peter to fix my car.（我叫 Peter 修理我的車子。）

　　意思都是一樣：我叫（使、讓）Peter 修理我的車子。在英文文法上，把 Have、Make、Let 歸類為使役動詞，習慣上後面的動詞要用原形，即前面的 To 要省略，但 Get 因不列入使役動詞，所以後面的動詞前，不能把 To 省略，因此上面的句子要改成：

I had Peter fix my car.

I made Peter fix my car.

I let Peter fix my car.

I got Peter <u>to fix</u> my car.

此類句子的句構是：

Have
Make
Let

}：不完全及物動詞＋受詞（人）＋原形動詞做
受詞

Get：不完全及物動詞＋受詞（人）＋不定詞片語做受詞
補語

這類句子也可以把 My car 放到前面來變成：

I had my car fixed by Peter.

I made my car fixed by Peter.

I let my car fixed by Peter.

I got my car fixed by Peter.

意思都一樣：我使（讓）我的車子被 Peter 修理。再舉
一例說明這種英文句型的用法，我們去美容院請人家幫
我們洗頭髮，英文寫成：

I had someone wash my hair.（我叫某人洗我的頭髮。）

I made someone wash my hair.

I let someone wash my hair.

I got someone <u>to wash</u> my hair.

或：

I had my hair washed by someone.

I made my hair washed by someone.

I let my hair washed by someone.

I got my hair washed by someone.

後者的句型是：

Have ⌐

Make ｜：不完全及物動詞＋受詞（事物）＋過去分詞

Let ｜　　做受詞補語

Get ⌐

現在我們回到本文，我們寫信要求 Buyer 叫銀行開發信用狀，To have the L/C opened 即由 To have your bank open the L/C 變成 To have the L/C opened by your bank，而把 by your bank 省略掉。

8. Appreciate：（感激）相當於 Thank you for，所以 Appreciate 後面不必再加 For，只要直接加上感激的事物即可。

第二種理由

■ 範　例

如第一種理由的範例，只是將

In order to book the shipping space at an earlier date.

改成：In order to arrange production in due course.

翻譯

為了要在適當的時候安排生產。

⊚ 解說

In due course：（在適當的時候）

第三種理由

■ 範　例

（上下文請參照第一種理由的範例。）

Goods are ready for shipment. You are requested to have the L/C opened immediately so that we may ship the goods in July as contracted.

⊚ 翻譯

貨品已準備好要裝運，請您立刻開發信用狀，以便我們依合約規定在七月分出貨。

⊚ 解說

1. Goods are ready：（貨品已準備好了）也可以用 Goods are prepared 代替，人準備好了也可以用 Ready，例如：I am ready to go now.（我已準備現在要走了。）

2. As contracted：（依合約）這是副詞片語。Contract 當名詞用時是（合約），當動詞用時是（訂合約）或（簽約）。此處的 Contracted 是過去分詞，這種句構來自於 As，也可以作為像關係代名詞 Which 一樣，用來修飾主要子句。

例如：

She is pretty which is known to us.

＝ She is pretty as is known to us.

（她人很漂亮我們都知道。）

本文中 We may ship the goods in July as contracted.

＝ We may ship the goods in July as was contracted.

＝ We may ship the goods in July which was contracted.

（我們可以依合約規定在七月分出貨。）

Which 後面的 Be 動詞可以省略，所以變成 As contracted。此種用法常見的有：As requested（依要求）、As instructed（依指示）、As specified（依指定）、As mentioned（依提到的）。

例如：

We will send you samples as requested.

＝ We will send you samples as were requested.

＝ We will send you samples which were requested.

（我們將依要求寄給您樣品。）

省略 Be 動詞 Were 之後，就變成 As requested。

第四種理由

▌範　例

（上下文請參照第一種理由的範例。）

Makers here will not proceed with any order until the arrival of the L/C for fear of possible cancellation.

翻譯

這邊的廠商在信用狀沒到之前，不會著手處理任何訂單，因爲擔心訂單可能被取消。

解說

1. Maker：（廠商）等於 Manufacturer，但 Maker 較偏重於所生產的產品，手工成分占一半左右的工廠，例如：手錶工廠叫做 Watch-maker、鞋子工廠叫做 Shoe-maker，因爲手錶及鞋子在生產過程中，使用手工的部分很多。

   如果產品大部分是用機器製造的，則用 Manufacturer，一般來說 Manufacturer 規模較大。

2. Proceed with：（著手處理、進行處理）

   例如：Let us proceed with our research.（讓我們著手做研究。）

   另 Proceed to 是（前進）的意思。

   例如：Let us proceed to page 2.（讓我們進行到第二頁。）

3. For fear of possible cancellation：（因爲擔心可能取消）
   For 在此處是表示原因的介系詞，後面接名詞當受詞，如果後
   面要接子句當受詞時，等於連接詞的 Because，只不過 For 表
   達原因的程度，沒有 Because 那樣強烈。

Unit 2　無法如期出貨要求延期的事實或藉口

說明

　　訂單在生產期間，往往會受到各種因素的影響，而無法依照約定準時交貨，因此要求客戶延期，為了讓客戶諒解及答應，我們所提的理由或藉口，其文辭語意一定要很有說服力，才能達到目的。

　　過去二、三十年來，我們的廠商一碰到無法如期出貨時，不是說工廠遭受火災就是水災，以致國外的 Buyer 已不再相信這樣的說辭了。

　　在這裡我們列舉六種不同的藉口供業者參考。

第一種藉口

範　例

　　In fact, a terrible typhoon struck this part of the country on the 5th this month and our factory suffered serious damage making it impossible to ship your order within the validity of the subject L/C.

Under the circumstances, we hope you will understand the situation and agree to extend the credit till Sept. 30.

We will do everything in our power to expedite manufacture. The expected date of shipment will be around Sept. 15.

⌖ 翻譯

　　事實上，一個可怕的颱風，在本月 5 日侵襲我們這個地方，而且我們的工廠遭受到嚴重的損害，以致於造成要在信用狀的有效期內，出您的訂單已不可能。

　　在此情況下，我們希望您會了解這種情形，而且同意把信用狀延至 9 月 30 日，我們會盡一切所能加緊生產，預定的裝船日期將在 9 月 15 日左右。

⌖ 解說

1. In fact：（事實上）歐洲（尤其是英國）慣用 As a matter of fact。

2. Struck：是動詞 Strike（打擊）的過去式，此處做（侵襲）解釋。

3. This part of the country：（我們國家的這個地區），例如：臺灣的北部地區寫成 Northern part of Taiwan、中部地區寫成 Central part of Taiwan。

4. Our factory suffered serious damage making it impossible to ship your order within the validity of the subject L/C.
   此處的 It 是 Make 的虛受詞，真的受詞是後面的不定詞片語

To ship your order within the validity of the subject L/C.

◦ 補充說明 ◦

4-1. Make 表（使……成為……）時，是不完全及物動詞，不可以用不定詞片語做受詞，一定要用虛受詞 It 代替，其句型如下：

主詞＋ Make ＋ It ＋受詞補語＋ To

例如：I think <u>it</u> wrong <u>to tell lies</u>.

（我認為說謊是不對的。）

It 是 Think 的虛受詞，不定詞片語 To tell lies 才是真受詞。

4-2. Think、Consider、Believe、Find 做不完全及物動詞時，用法與 Make 相同。

4-3. 既然有假（虛）受詞，那麼是否有假（虛）主詞？有的。

例如：<u>It</u> is a bad habit <u>to waste money</u>.

　　假主詞　　　　　真主詞

（浪費金錢是一種壞習慣。）

當主詞過長時，往往使用 It 放在句子前面做主詞，而把真正的主詞放到後面。

又如：It is interesting to travel abroad.

4-4. Make 表（做）什麼時，是完全及物動詞。

例如：He made a kite.（他做了一個風箏。）

5. The subject L/C：（主旨提到的信用狀）

商業英文書信一般都有主旨，有人用 Reference（簡寫 Re），也有人用 Subject（簡寫 Subj 或 Sub）。

例如：Subj: L/C No.123 for US$10,000 covering order No.456.

當我們寫信的內容中，要再提到上述的信用狀時，就用 The subject L/C 就可以了，不必再重複 "L/C No.123 for US$10,000 covering order No.456" 這麼長，浪費時間。

> **補充說明**
>
> 我們常見到 Be + Subject to 的片語，做（聽命於、須以……為條件）的意思。
>
> 例如：This quotation is subject to our final confirmation.
> 〔此報價單聽候（命）於我們最後的確認。〕

信用狀最後一段，通常會寫上：

This credit is <u>subject to</u> Uniform Customs and Practice for Documentary Credits (2007 revision) International Chamber of Commerce, Publication No.600.

（本信用狀聽候於國際商會 2007 年修訂的信用狀統一慣例，第 600 號出版本。）

信用狀會加上這一句，主要的原因是由於信用狀統一慣例並非法律，制定或修訂機關——「國際商會」僅為一民間機構，不具強制性。L/C 基本架構係依當事人（L/C 的申請人、開狀銀行、受益人、押匯銀行）的意思，決定是否採用，共同遵守 L/C 有關條款的規定，因此開狀銀行於開發 L/C 時，會在信用狀下方上，表示 "The credit is subject to UCP 600"（本 L/C 係依據 UCP 600 而開發），以增強信用狀統一慣例的適用性，一旦有爭議時，就可以作為國際間處理信用狀業務的統一規則及依據。

6. Under the circumstances：（在這種情況下）

7. The credit：外國人通常把 Letter of credit 簡寫成 The credit，就好像我們把信用狀簡稱 L/C 一樣。

8. Do everything in our power：（盡一切力量）

9. Expedite：（加緊、加速）＝ Speed up

10. Around Sep. 15：訂單或 L/C 上面，如果日期前面有 Around 時，表示前後五天都可以接受，等於 On or about。

本文中預定的出貨日期是 9 月 15 日左右，廠商在 9 月 10 日及 20 日之間，任何一天出貨都符合規定，押匯時不會被認定有瑕疵。

第二種藉口

▌範　例

We are unable to ship the goods accordingly because of a recent fire at our factory which has nearly destroyed all our stocks.

翻譯

我們無法依規定出貨，因為最近發生在我們工廠的火災，幾乎燒毀了我們所有的存貨。

解說

本文這一句很長，可以把它分成二句如下：

We are unable to ship the goods accordingly because of a recent fire at our factory. It has nearly destroyed all our stocks.

（我們無法依規定出貨，因為工廠最近著火，這個火災幾乎毀掉我們所有的存貨。）

書信講求的是流暢而且連貫，不像口語那樣簡短，因此文法創造出關係代名詞，用來達成這個功能，關係代名詞兼有連接詞與代名詞的作用，可以把兩個句子連接起來，同時又可以代替名詞。關係代名詞有 Which、Who、That、Whose 等。

例如：He bought a car. It is very good.

　　　（他買了一部車子，它很好。）

　＝ He bought a car which is very good.

　　　（他買了一部很好的車子。）

　 I know the girl. She came yesterday.

　　（我認識這個女孩，她昨天來過。）

　＝ I know the girl who came yesterday.

　　　（我認識昨天來的那個女孩。）

由此可看出，有關係代名詞把兩個句子串聯起來，文辭顯得更為流暢。

第三種藉口

▌範　例

　　We are unable to ship the goods accordingly due to lack of space of the carrying vessel.

　　（下文請參照第一種藉口的範例。）

翻譯

　　我們無法依規定出貨，由於所要裝貨的船缺乏艙位。

解說

1. Due to：（由於……）做介系詞用。

2. Lack of space：（缺乏艙位）＝ Shortage of space

3. The carrying vessel：Vessel 前面加上 Carrying，表示我們所要裝貨的那條船，如果不加的話，那就變成任何一條船都缺乏艙位，沒有特定的對象。

　　船公司艙位不足，當然會影響到我們出貨。

第四種藉口

▌範　例

　　We are unable to ship the goods accordingly due to shortage of raw materials.

翻譯

我們無法依規定出貨，由於原料缺乏（不足）。

解說

原料不足時會影響生產進度，造成不是整批貨 Delay，就是要分批裝運出口（Partial shipments）。

第五種藉口

▌ 範 例

We are very sorry for the delay in the execution of your order. This delay is entirely attributable to the recent strike.
（下文請參照第一種藉口的範例。）

翻譯

我們很抱歉，在執行您的訂單時發生延誤，這個延誤完全歸因於最近的罷工。

解說

1. In the execution of：（執行）介系詞片語。
   原式動詞 Execute（執行），執行祕書是 Executive secretary。
   In the execution of your order 執行您的訂單，換句話說，就是生產您的訂單。
2. Entirely：（完全地）＝ Completely

3. This delay is entirely attributable to the recent strike.

（這個延誤完全歸因於最近的罷工。）

Is attributable to：（歸咎於、歸因於）相當於 Attribute to（把……歸因於……）

例如：Our factory attributes this delay to recent strike.

（我們的工廠把延誤歸咎於最近的罷工。）

Peter attributes success to his coach.

（Peter 把成功歸因於他的教練。）

第六種藉口

▌範　例

We are unable to ship the goods accordingly because of breakdown in factory machinery.

（下文請參照第一種藉口的範例。）

◎ 翻譯

我們無法如期出貨，因為工廠的機器故障。

◎ 解說

1. Because of：（因為、由於）＝ Due to

2. Breakdown：（故障）

3. Machinery：（機器）是商品的集合名詞，與 Machine 有區別，描述整體機器叫做 Machinery。

例如：Mass production needs a great deal of machinery.
　　　（大量生產需要很多機器。）

個別的機器則稱 Machine，例如：Sewing machine（縫紉機）、
Washing machine（洗衣機）。
其他商品的集合名詞，諸如 General merchandise（雜貨）、
Hardware（五金）、Footwear（鞋子）、Furniture（傢俱）等。

Unit 3　要求修改 L/C

 說明

　　接到信用狀，一定要先仔細檢查內容是否與我們當初簽訂的條件一致，亦即交貨條件、數量、價格、金額、出貨日期、保險條款及信用狀到期日等，如果其中任何一項有誤或做不到，就應儘速告訴 Buyer 進行修改，以免到時來不及處理。

　　最常碰到的問題有下列幾項。

第一項　無法準時交貨，要求延期並修改 L/C

範　例

　　Regret to inform you that the first available vessel to Hamburg is scheduled to leave here on or about July 15. Since the latest shipment date as specified in the subject L/C is July 10, we are unable to ship the goods before the deadline.

　　Under the circumstances, we hereby request you to have both the date of shipment and the expiry date of the L/C extended to August 15 and August 30 respectively.

◎ 翻譯

　　很遺憾通知您，我們要裝貨的第一班到漢堡的船，預定在 7 月 15 日左右啟航，因為在主旨上所提到的信用狀，規定最遲裝船日期是 7 月 10 日，我們無法在限期之前出貨。

　　在這種情況下，我們藉此請求您，把裝船日期及信用狀的到期日，分別延至 8 月 15 日及 8 月 30 日。

◎ 解說

1. The first available vessel to Hamburg 與 The first vessel to Hamburg 有點不同，前者在 Vessel 之前加上 Available，意思是我們所要利用的第一班到漢堡的船，也就是我們要裝貨的船，而後者是第一班到漢堡的船（不一定是我們要裝貨的船），因此在 Vessel 之前，加上 Available 更能表達我們的意思。
   其用法猶如在單元二中所提到的 The carrying vessel，Vessel 之前加上 Carrying，表示我們要裝貨的那條船。

2. Is scheduled to：（行程預定）
   交通工具如汽車、火車、輪船及飛機等的行程預定，人的行程預定亦同。
   例如：He is scheduled to visit Germany next week.
   　　　（他預定下星期訪問德國。）

3. Leave：（離開、啟航）＝ Depart ＝ Sail

4. Since：（因為）此處是表示原因的連接詞，同類的有 Because、As、For，依表達原因強弱的程度，依序為 Because、Since、As、For。

補充說明

Since 亦可作為表示時間的介系詞（自從、自……以來），表示某件事情繼續到現在的起點，常和完成式連用。

例如：Our company has been established since 1960.

（我們公司自從 1960 年就已設立。）

From 也是表示時間的介系詞（自從），表示起點。

例如：I lived in London from 1960 to 1965.

（自 1960 年到 1965 年我住在倫敦。）

5. Deadline：（最後期限）

此處表示 L/C 規定的最遲裝船日期 July 10。

第二項　由於船公司缺乏艙位無法一次出完，要求修改 L/C

範　例

Much to our regret, we could not deliver the total quantity by one shipment for lack of space of the carrying vessel. Please amend L/C to allow partial shipments.

At the same time, please have both the date of shipment and the expiry date of the L/C extended to August 15 and August 30 respectively.

翻譯

我們深感遺憾，無法把整個數量一次交清，因為我們所要裝貨的船缺乏艙位。請修改信用狀，允許分批出貨，並且把裝船日期及信用狀到期日，分別延至8月15日及8月30日。

解說

By one shipment：（一次出清）

＝ By one lot，亦即不准 Partial shipments 分批裝運（出貨）。

第三項　保險條款無法做到，要求修改 L/C

範　例

Thank you for your L/C No.123 of the Bank of London covering your order No.456. We find it in order except the insurance clause reading "Against all risks from any cause". We negotiated with the underwriters but learned that they would not insure the goods against such extensive risks. We would ask you to amend the L/C by replacing the stipulation with "ICC (B) including war risks and TPND".

翻譯

謝謝您倫敦銀行開來的第 123 號信用狀，此信用狀是涵蓋您的第 456 號訂單，我們發現其內容除了保險條款之外，都沒有問題，保險條款如是說「針對任何原因的所有風險」，

我們與保險公司洽談過，得知他們將不針對如此密集的風險
承保貨物。

　　我們請您修改信用狀，用「協會貨物保險 B 條款加上附
加險的兵險及偷竊遺失險」，來取代原保險條款。

✎ 解說

1. In order：此處等於 In good order（合乎規則地），另一解釋爲
   （安然）等於 Safely。

   例如：The books arrived in good order.

   　　　（那些書安然無損地到達。）

   ┌─── 補充說明 ───┐

   In order to ＋動詞（爲了……，以便……）

   這比單用 To 不定詞，或 So as to ＋動詞，更能強調目的
   的觀念，爲正式的表達法。（用 To 或 So as to 較不正式）

   例如：He will visit Germany in order to attend a meeting.

   　　　（他將造訪德國爲了參加一項會議。）

2. We find it in order except the insurance clause reading "…".：

   （我們發現其內容除了保險條款之外，都沒問題，保險條款
   如是說「……」。）

   Reading 前面省略 Which，這個 Which 關係代名詞，是修飾前
   面的前述詞 Insurance clause。全句如下：

   We find it in order except the <u>insurance clause</u> which reads "…".

> ◦ **補充說明** ◦
>
> 當關係代名詞做主詞時，其後引導的形容詞子句可以化
> 簡為分詞片語，其法則如下：
> a. 刪除該關係代名詞。
> b. 其後的動詞變成現在分詞。
> c. 若動詞為 Be 動詞可以省略。

例如：The man who was reading a newspaper in the sitting room
did not hear the accident.

＝ The man reading a newspaper in the sitting room did not
hear the accident.

（在起居室看報紙的男人，沒有聽到這個意外。）

I know the boy who is crossing the street.

＝ I know the boy crossing the street.

（我認識正在過馬路的那位男孩。）

3. Against all risks from any cause：（針對任何原因的所有風
險）在商業英文中，Against 做（針對）解釋，如 Against your
order（針對您的訂單）、Against your L/C（針對您的信用狀）。

4. Underwriter：（保險商）＝ Insurance company

5. We would ask you：（我們請求您）
此處的 Would 不是過去的未來式，而是表示客氣的用法，例
如：我們請朋友吃飯，要點什麼，如果用 What do you want to
eat? 這樣不太禮貌，如用 What would you like to have? 就客氣
多了。

6. To amend the L/C by replacing the stipulation with "ICC (B) including war risks and TPND."：（修改信用狀，用 ICC (B) 條款並含兵險及偷竊遺失險，來取代原條款。）

6-1. By：是（藉）

6-2. Replace：動詞（代替）

例如：They have replaced their old car with (by) a new one.
（他們以一部新車更換了舊車。）

另一同義字是 Substitute：（代替）

例如：Substitute margarine for butter.
（以人造奶油代替奶油。）

此二字在使用時要注意：

Replace A with（或 By）B. 是（用 B 取代 A。）

Substitute A for B. 是（用 A 取代 B。）

例如：

The old typewriters are being replaced by new ones.
（新打字機替換舊打字機。）

＝ New typewriters are being substituted for the old.

6-3. ICC (B)：基本險中的 B 條款

＝ Institute cargo clauses (B)
（協會貨物保險 B 條款）

其保障範圍大於 ICC (C) 條款，但小於 ICC (A) 條款。

6-4. TPND：Theft、Pilferage、Non-delivery
附加險中的一種（偷竊、剽竊及遺失）

第四項　信用狀金額不符，要求修改 L/C

▌範　例

　　We find that the L/C amount for US$ 8,000 is inconsistent with that listed in our Sales Confirmation No. 345. The correct amount should be US$ 8,500.

翻譯

　　我們發現信用狀的金額美金 8,000 元，與我們第 345 號的銷售合約（確認書）所列的金額不符，正確的金額應為美金 8,500 元。

解說

1. For US$8,000：金額前面的介系詞大都用 For。
2. Is inconsistent with：（與……不一致）
   ＝ Does not agree with
3. That listed in our Sales Confirmation No.345：
   That 代替 Amount，一個句子中最好避免重複同樣的字。

Unit

4　向船公司索賠的信函

🔒 說 明

　　貨主提貨時，發現貨物有短少或破損，要立刻通知承運的船公司，或其代理商（先口頭告知，再補上書面文件）。在法律上，當貨物毀損、滅失很明顯時，貨主要在提貨當天或之前通知運送人，但毀損或滅失不明顯時，例如：外箱受扭曲破損，但不知裡面的貨物是否毀損／滅失，其程度狀況不明確時，可以在交貨後三日內通知運送人，否則運送人可以依法不受理。

　　由於國內的空運公司或船務代理公司，大多代理國外的航空公司或船公司，如 KLM、MP、CV、NYK、P&O 及 MAERSK 等，他們往往要求貨主提供英文的書面索賠信函，以便寄送船東瞭解及處理。

　　索賠信函分二階段進行，第一階段先發索賠通知，第二階段俟公證行把毀損／滅失的細節做成公證報告，而且已算出損失（賠償）金額時，再寫一封索賠信函，連同公證報告，並附上相關的裝船文件給船公司（或航空公司），這時索賠的動作才暫告一段落。

第一項　索賠通知書

▌範　例

RE: NOTICE OF CLAIM　　OUR REFERENCE: _____

　　　VESSEL: _____　　VOYAGE NO.: _____

　　　B/L NO.: _____　　B/L DATE: _____

　　　FROM/TO: _____

　　　　　　　　　　(details of shipment)

Dear Sirs,

　　We have been informed that the above shipment arrived at destination in damaged condition/with shortage. We must therefore hold you fully responsible for the damage/loss incurred.

　　Our goods were delivered into the charge of your CFS on ____ date in good condition. Obviously the cargo was damaged during the carriage. (in full quantity. Obviously cargo was missing during the carriage.)

　　Please be advised that we reserve all rights on behalf of cargo owner and their underwriters to file a claim with you when details of damage/loss have been ascertained.

Yours faithfully,

_____

CC: Consignee (Buyer)

註：如要寫給空運公司，只要將 Vessel 改成 Carrier，Voyage No. 改成 Flight No. 然後略加修改即可。

🎯 翻譯

主旨：索賠通知書　　　我們的編號：＿＿＿＿＿＿

　　　船名：＿＿＿＿＿＿　航次：＿＿＿＿＿＿＿

　　　提單號碼：＿＿＿＿　提單日期：＿＿＿＿

　　　從何處啟運至何目的地：＿＿＿＿＿＿＿＿＿

　　　（貨物名稱、有幾箱等細節）

敬啟者：

　　我們被告知，上面這批貨到目的地時，是毀損的狀況（或滅失），所以我們必須要貴公司負起這已發生的毀損（或滅失）的全部責任。

　　我們的貨在某年某月某日是完好的狀況下，送到貨櫃場的 CFS 倉，由你們接管，很顯然的，貨物是在運送途中受到毀損。（如果是貨物短缺，此句要改成──我們的貨在某年某月某日以完整的數量送進貨櫃場由你們接管，很明顯的這些貨是在運送途中不見了。）

　　請知悉，我們代表貨主及他們的保險公司，保留所有的權利，當毀損／滅失的細節被確定時，我們將向貴公司提出索賠。

◎ 解說

1. In damaged condition：（毀損的狀況）此處的 Damaged 是 Damage 的過去分詞，當形容詞使用，修飾 Condition。

2. Hold you fully responsible for：要你負責，寫成 Hold you responsible，負什麼責任的介系詞要用 For。Fully 是副詞，修飾 Responsible 強調負全責之意。

3. Our goods were delivered into the charge of your CFS：

    3-1.　CFS 是 Container freight station（貨櫃貨物集散站）。在貨櫃場內的倉庫，貨物在此併櫃或拆櫃，由於併櫃貨（Less than container load）縮寫為 LCL，是貨主用卡車送來此處裝櫃，所以把 LCL 貨也叫做 CFS 貨。

    3-2.　Charge：在此處是做名詞（保管、照料）之意。
    　　　例如：The baby was left in the charge of the neighbor.
    　　　（這嬰兒被留給鄰居照料。）

4. During the carriage：（在運送途中）亦即在運輸的過程中，等於 In transit。
    Carriage 亦可用 Transportation 代替。
    例如：The goods were damaged in transit.
    　　　（商品在運送途中破損了。）

5. On behalf of：（代表某人）

6. Cargo owner：（貨主）船務實務上，誰握有 B/L 誰就擁有提貨權，他就是貨主。

7. File a claim with you：（向您提出索賠）
    File 也可用 Lodge 代替。

第二項　索賠請求書

範　例

RE: NOTE OF CLAIM　　OUR REFERENCE: _____

　　VESSEL: _____ VOYAGE NO.: _____

　　B/L NO.: _____B/L DATE: _____FROM/TO: _____

(details of shipment)
_____

CLAIMED AMOUNT: US$_____

Dear Sirs,

Please refer to our notice of claim ref. no. _____ dated_____, we are enclosing herewith the following related copies of documents for your reference:

　　1) B/L copy

　　2) Commercial invoice

　　3) Packing list

　　4) Survey report

　　5) Pictures

You are kindly requested to reimburse us for the loss as mentioned above soon.

Yours faithfully,

_____

CC: Consignee (Buyer)

⊙ 翻譯

　　第二項範例的主旨如同第一項的索賠通知書範例，但此處多加一項 Claimed Amount（求償金額）。

　　其大致內容翻譯如下：

　　請參閱我們某年某月某日的索賠通知書，隨函附上下列有關的文件供參考：

　　1) 提單影本

　　2) 商業發票

　　3) 裝箱單

　　4) 公證報告

　　5) 相片

　　我們要求貴公司，儘速賠償我們上述所提的損失（即主旨上的求償金額）。

⊙ 解說

1.　Note of claim：（索賠請求書）＝ Letter of claim

2.　Claimed amount：（索賠的金額）亦即損害的金額。

3.　Related：（相關的）＝ Relative

4.　Survey report：（公證報告、鑑定報告）

　　Surveyor（勘察人、鑑定人、公證行）

5.　Reimburse：（賠償）

　　＝ Compensate，賠償某人的損失，後面加上介系詞 For。

　　例如：I reimbursed him for the losses.（我補償他的損失。）

Unit 5　因應客戶 Complaint 的回函

🔒 說 明

　　Buyer 抱怨的事情有很多種，諸如出貨延誤、Item 搞錯、品質不良、數量不足……，我們接到客戶的 Complaint 信函時，首先向他致歉意，並追查原因，然後再向 Buyer 報告問題所在，發生的原因為何。同時我們要儘快採取補救的措施，以減少客戶的不便及損失，並請客戶諒解。但假如調查的結果我們並沒有錯，可能是 Buyer 想藉機「揩油」撈點利益，我們必須回函據理力爭，以免 Buyer 將如法炮製得寸進尺。

第一項　Buyer 抱怨出貨延誤

範例一

　　The delay was entirely attributable to the recent strike and we regret that such a delay has been caused when you need the goods most urgently. In order to show you that we are anxious to avoid putting you to any further inconvenience, we have put aside other standing orders and have arranged to dispatch your goods by M.S. "President" leaving Keelung on May 5.

翻譯

　　這個延誤完全是由於最近的罷工所致，我們很遺憾在您急需這批貨品的時候，居然發生延誤情事。為了向您表示我們急於防止把您推向進一步的不方便，我們已經把別人固定的訂單擺在一邊（亦即專門生產您的訂單），而且我們也已安排好，會將您所訂的貨，裝載在 5 月 5 日將從基隆港啟航的「總統輪」。

解說

1. Avoid putting you to any further inconvenience：

　　（防止把您推向進一步的不方便）換句話說，就是速採補救措施，以免一延再延，造成 Buyer 更大的不便或損失。

　　此處的 Avoid 是及物動詞（防止），後面接動名詞 Putting 當受詞。

> **補充說明**
>
> 1-1. 並非所有的及物動詞，都可以接動名詞當受詞，有的及物動詞後面，只能接不定詞當受詞，常見的有 Want、Hope、Try、Intend、Expect、Decide、Like、Determine、Wish 等。

例如：I want to eat.（我要吃。）

　　　He plans to visit Europe.（他計劃造訪歐洲。）

名詞不定詞做及物動詞的受詞時，該及物動詞均為表示意願、企圖、目的或未完成的事之動詞。

┌─○　補充說明　○─────────────┐

　1-2.　常見以動名詞做受詞的動詞有：

　　　　Avoid（避免）、Mind（介意）、Enjoy（喜歡）、Practice（練習）、Finish（完成）、Deny（否認）、Recommend（推薦）、Suggest（建議）、Risk（冒險）等。

└───────────────────────┘

例如：I practice speaking English every morning.

　　　（我每天早上練習說英語。）

　　　She enjoys watching television.

　　　（她喜歡看電視。）

用動名詞做及物動詞的受詞時，該及物動詞均為表示經驗或已知的事。

2. Put aside：（放在一邊）

3. Other：（別人的）

4. Standing orders：（固定的訂單）

5. Dispatch：（發送、運送）

　Dispatch ＝ Ship ＝ Forward ＝ Send ＝ Deliver

6. Complain：（抱怨）是動詞，請注意其名詞是 Complaint。

■ 範例二

We are very sorry for the delay in the shipment of your order. This delay is due to causes beyond our control.

In order to show you that we are anxious...（下文請參照範例一。）

翻譯

我們很抱歉在出您的訂單時發生延誤，這個延誤是由於我們所無法控制的原因所造成，為了要向您表示我們急於……

解說

1. In the shipment of your order：（準備出您的訂單時）
   這與單元二中範例五的 In the execution of your order 不同，前者是訂單生產完後，準備要出貨的階段，而後者是訂單還在生產的過程。

2. Causes beyond our control：（我們無法控制的原因）如颱風、罷工……。

▌ 範例三

These goods were delayed in reaching container terminal from the plant due to traffic jam. Consequently they were shut out of the ship.

However, we have been doing everything possible in our power to deliver the goods by next available vessel within a week. In the meantime, we offer our apologies to you for the inconvenience the delay has caused you.

翻譯

這些貨從工廠運到貨櫃場時，因為交通壅塞延誤抵達，結果趕不及裝上船而退關。

然而我們已盡力安排下一班船，在一星期內出貨，同時我們對於這個延誤造成您的不便表示歉意。

解說

1. Plant：（工廠）＝ Factory
2. Traffic jam：（交通壅塞）＝ Traffic congestion
3. They were shut out of the ship：（貨沒有裝上船而退關）
   They 代表前句的 These goods，這裡所說的退關，係指貨沒有裝上這班船，必須先辦理退關，才可以再報關裝下班船，並不是貨物本身有問題，而遭致海關退關，所以本句不可寫成：
   They were shut out by customs.

否則 Buyer 一定會很疑惑，是不是您出的貨，品質有問題，海關檢查不合格，不讓這些貨物出口，或者這些貨是違禁品遭致擋關。

■ 範例四

　　We are very sorry for the delay in the shipment of your order as we have to obtain a special licence from authorities concerned to meet customs' requirement. （下文接 However, we have been doing...）

◎ 翻譯

　　我們很抱歉，在出您的訂單時發生延誤，因為我們必須向有關單位取得特別證照，來配合海關的要求。

◎ 解說

A special licence：（特殊證照）
例如：出口紡織品，要向紡拓會申請出口配額（Export visa），有些管制出口的商品，要向國貿局申請輸出許可證 （Export permit），有時申請作業來不及，可能會影響裝運出口。

第二項　貨品不符，Item 搞錯

範例一

Upon tracing we find that owing to the pressure of business, our shipping clerk shipped the goods of pattern No.2 instead of those of pattern No.1 for which your order was placed.

In order to adjust the matter, we ask you to accept the goods at an allowance of 20% though we sustain a great loss. As the price of No.1 is lower by 10% than that of No.2.

We sincerely regret that we have caused you inconvenience through our oversight. And we assure you that every effort will be made in future to prevent any repetition of such mistakes.

翻譯

在我們追查後，發現我們的船務人員，由於業務上的壓力，出了式樣 2 號的貨，而不是您所訂的式樣 1 號的貨。

為了要調整這件事情，我們想請您接受這些貨物，我們願意給您 20% 的折讓，雖然我們遭受很大的損失，因為式樣 1 號的價錢比式樣 2 號便宜 10%。

我們很遺憾由於我方一時的疏忽，造成您不方便。我們要向您保證，我們將盡力防止類似的錯誤再發生。

⊙ 解說

1. Upon tracing：（一調查後就……）Tracing 的原形動詞是
    Trace（追蹤、調查），後面加上 ing 成為動名詞，是因為前
    面有介系詞 Upon 的關係。

    ┌─── ∘ 補充說明 ∘ ───┐

    Upon ┐　＋名詞／動名詞＋主要子句
    On 　┘　＝ As soon as ＋副詞子句＋主要子句

    翻譯成：一……就……

    例如：On seeing the policeman, the juvenile delinquents
    　　　ran away.

    　　　（一看到警察，不良少年就跑掉了。）

    　　＝ As soon as the juvenile delinquents saw the
    　　　　policeman, they ran away.

    └────────────────────┘

2. Owing to：（由於……）＝ Due to

3. Pressure of business：（業務上的壓力）

4. Instead of：（而不是）

5. Those：代替 The goods。

6. Pattern No.1 for which your order was placed.

    ＝ Pattern No.1 which your order was placed for.

    Which 修飾前述詞 Pattern No.1，而介系詞 For 本應放在 Place
    後面，但習慣上一個句子中有關係代名詞時，其句尾的介系
    詞，大都放在關係代名詞的前面。

    Place order for 意思是（下訂單購買……）。

例如：He placed an order for 500 pieces of wooden chairs.
（他下訂單購買 500 張木椅。）

而 Place order with 是（向某人或某公司下訂單）。

7. Allowance：（折讓）

8. Though：＝ Although（雖然……但是……）

例如：Though ⌉ Peter is a good student,
　　　Although ⌋ I do not like him.

（雖然 Peter 是一位好學生，但是我不喜歡他。）

這句話我們很容易直接用中文翻成英文而寫成：

Though ⌉ Peter is a good student, <u>but</u>
Although ⌋ I do not like him.

這是錯誤的，因為 Though 本身已是連接詞，But 也是連接詞，一個句子當中要避免雙重連接，因此正確的寫法應為：

Though Peter is a good student, I do not like him.

或 Peter is a good student, but I do not like him.

又如：Because Mary is a nice girl, so I like her.
（因為 Mary 是好女孩，所以我喜歡她。）

這也是錯誤的寫法，Because 與 So 都是連接詞，因此要改為：

Because Mary is a nice girl, I like her.

或 Mary is a nice girl, so I like her.

有 Because 就不要再加上 So，或有 So 就不要再加 Because。

┌───┐
○ **補充說明** ○

任何一個副詞連接詞所引導的子句，若放在主句後面，
兩句間通常不加逗點，但假如該副詞子句放在主句前
面，則兩句間要加逗點。
└───┘

例如上面的例子：

Because Mary is a nice girl, I like her.

＝ I like her because Mary is a nice girl.

Though Peter is a good student, I don't like him.

＝ I don't like him though Peter is a good student.

常用的副詞連接詞有下列幾個：

But、If、Though、Because、Unless、When、Once、So、As
soon as 等。

▌範例二

Upon tracing we find that the mistake occurred in our
forwarding department and was due to our reorganization
program.

We have shipped today the replacement for the
different goods of which you complained in your letter of
July 15.

We apologize deeply for this most regrettable mistake
and have taken proper measures to prevent recurrence of
similar errors in the future.

翻譯

　　經調查後，我們發現這個錯誤，發生在我們的運送部門，而且是由於我們重組的計劃所致。

　　我們已在今天運出代替品，取代您在 7 月 15 日信上所抱怨的那些不同的東西。

　　我們為這個不幸的錯誤，深深地向您致歉，我們已採取適當的措施，來防止將來類似的錯誤再發生。

解說

1.　Replacement：（替代品）後面的介系詞 For，接被取代的東西。

2.　The different goods of which you complained in your letter.

　　= The different goods which you complained of in your letter.

　　（您信上所抱怨的那些不同的東西。）

關係代名詞 Which，修飾前述詞 The different goods，介系詞 Of 本來是擺在 Complained 的後面，然後再接抱怨的事物。

例如：The child complained of hunger and thirst.

　　　　（這小孩抱怨又餓又渴。）

因為 Complain 本身是不及物動詞，後面如要接名詞做受詞時，一定要先加介系詞 Of，否則就要用 Complain that ＋子句的型態。

例如：He complains that his job gives him no satisfaction.

　　　　（他抱怨他的工作不能滿足他。）

┌─────────── ∘ 補充說明 ∘ ───────────┐

使用關係代名詞要記住下列三個條件：

a. 關係代名詞之前，要有前述詞（或稱先行詞，即人或事物的名詞）。

b. 關係代名詞在所引導的形容詞子句中，要做主詞、受詞或 Be 動詞的補語。

c. 否則關係代名詞之前，一定要有介系詞。

└────────────────────────────────┘

例如：He is the boy who cleaned the window.

（他就是清洗窗子的那個男孩。）

Who 之前有前述詞 The boy，Who 在所引導的子句中做主詞，其後有動詞 Cleaned 及受詞 Window。

This is the book which I bought yesterday.

（這是我昨天所買的書。）

The book 是 Which 的前述詞，Which 在所引導的形容詞子句中，做及物動詞 Bought 的受詞。

The city which he lives is very big.（×）

（他所居住的城市很大。）

這是錯誤的，雖然 Which 之前有前述詞 The city，但所引導的子句中，已有主詞 He，而且 Live 為不及物動詞，Which 不能做受詞，既然 Which 不能做主詞，也不能做受詞，所以這是錯誤的句構，這時 Which 之前就應放介系詞，改為：

The city in which he lives is very big.（○）

2-1. 關係代名詞之前有介系詞時，介系詞可移到所引導的形容
　　　詞子句句尾，此時可省略關係代名詞。

　　　例如：The city in which he lives is very big.

　　　　　　＝ The city which he lives in is very big.

　　　　　　＝ The city he lives in is very big.

　　　把介系詞 In 放到後面，關係代名詞 Which 可省略。

　　　又如：The woman about whom you were talking is my aunt.

　　　　　　（你正談到的女人是我的姨媽。）

　　　　　　＝ The woman whom you were talking about is my aunt.

　　　　　　＝ The woman you were talking about is my aunt.

　　　把介系詞 About 放到後面，同時將關係代名詞 Whom 省略。

2-2. 關係代名詞又可分為限定修飾及非限定修飾的用法，使用
　　　在限定用法的句子中，前面不要加逗點，如果使用在非限
　　　定時，關係代名詞前面要加逗點。

　　　所謂非限定修飾的用法，就是關係代名詞前面的前述詞，
　　　如果是專有名詞，如 Peter、Mary、Judy、London、Taipei
　　　或獨一性名詞，如 Husband、Father、Wife、Mother，其本
　　　身就具有特殊性，不必再用形容詞子句加以限定。

　　　例如：I sent it to Jones, who passed it on to Smith.

　　　　　　（我把它送給 Jones，而他把它給了 Smith。）

　　　Jones 本身已是特定的人，不必再藉關係代名詞 Who 來加以
　　　形容。而限定修飾的用法，就是關係代名詞前面的前述詞，
　　　如果是一般名詞，本身並不具特殊性，可用關係代名詞所
　　　引導的形容詞子句，加以限定修飾，以加強其特殊性。

　　　　例如：He is the boy who broke the window.

　　　　　　（他就是打破窗子的那個男孩。）

前述詞 The boy 並沒有獨特性，但經過 Who 所引導的形容詞子句加以修飾之後，就成為限定的人了，亦即本句中打破窗子的那個男孩。

現在我們來注意下列兩例有關限定用法與非限定用法的差別：

a-1.　He had two daughters who became nurses.　——限定用法

（他有兩個當了護士的女兒。）意謂他不只有兩個女兒，其餘的女兒不是護士。

a-2.　He had two daughters, who became nurses.　——非限定用法

（他有兩個女兒，她們都當了護士。）意謂他總共有兩個女兒。

b-1.　Her husband, who is living in Japan often writes to her.

（她的丈夫現在住在日本，時常寫信給她。）意謂她只有一個丈夫。

b-2.　Her husband who is living in Japan often writes to her.

（她住在日本的丈夫，時常寫信給她。）意謂她不只有一個丈夫。

用了限定用法，就變成她有兩個以上的丈夫了。

第三項　貨物品質不良

▊ 範例一

We have received your letter of July 15 and must apologize for sending you the goods of inferior quality. To put the matter right we will ship replacements next week for all the items you have found unsatisfactory, and would ask you to send us by air at our expense two each of the goods for our factory manager to examine.

翻譯

我們已接到您 7 月 15 日的來信，我們對於出了品質不良的貨，向您道歉，為了調整這件事情，我們將在下星期裝運代替品給您，取代所有您認為不滿意的貨品，同時希望您用航空寄給我們每種貨品兩件，費用由我方負擔，以便我們工廠經理做檢查。

解說

1. Inferior：（較劣的、較差的）

2. Put...right：（調整、改正）＝ Adjust

3. All the items you have found unsatisfactory. （所有您發現不滿意的貨品。）

   Items 後面省略關係代名詞 Which，因為 Which 是 Found 動詞的受格。

＝ All the items which you have found unsatisfactory.

```
○── 補充說明 ──○
```

凡受格關係代名詞 Whom、Which、That，如用做及物
動詞或介系詞的受詞時可以省略，但有介系詞在關係代
名詞前面時除外。

例如：This is the book which（或 that）I bought yesterday.

（這是我昨天買的書。）

The book 做 Bought 的受詞，所以 Which 是受格，可以
省略。

＝ This is the book I bought yesterday.

又如：She is the girl whom we are looking for.

（她就是我們正在找的女孩。）

The girl 作為介系詞 For 的受詞，所以 Whom 關係代名
詞受格可以省略。

＝ She is the girl we are looking for.

4. Unsatisfactory：（不滿意的）形容詞，在此當受詞補語，其句
型如下：

All the items which you have found unsatisfactory.

＝ All the items you have found unsatisfactory.

＝ You have found <u>all the items</u> <u>unsatisfactory</u>.

　　　　　　　　　受詞　　　受詞補語

5. At our expense：（由我方付費）＝ For our account

國外開來的 L/C，經常會有如下列的註明：

All banking charges outside France（或其他地方）are for beneficiary's account.（或 for the account of the beneficiary）

（所有銀行的費用，在法國之外，全由受益人負擔。）

＝ All banking charges outside France are at beneficiary's expense.

6. Two each of the goods：Two 後面省略 Pieces（件）

　　例如：One piece each of the goods.（每種貨品一件。）

　　　　　＝ One each of the goods.

7. Agree to your selling the remainder：（同意您來銷售剩餘的商品）

　　Agree to（同意）是動詞片語，此處的 To 是介系詞，所以後面 Sell 要用動名詞 Selling，同時 You 要用所有格 Your 才符合文法。

　　例如：I agree to your point.（我同意你的觀點。）

　　　　　Point 是 To 介系詞的名詞受詞，而本文中的 Agree to your selling... 則用動名詞 Selling 做介系詞 To 的受詞。

　　習慣上 Agree with 用於對人或事，Agree to 用於對事。

8. Remainder：（剩下的東西或人）

　　＝ The rest ＝ Balance

▋範例二

　　We are sorry to learn that you are not satisfied with the goods supplied to your order No.123. You claimed that quality was inferior to the original sample. This does not appear to be very reasonable as we sent you an advance sample prior to shipment and did not hear from you to the contrary.

　　Presumed it to be in order.

☉ 翻譯

我們很遺憾得知，您對我們供應給您第 123 號訂單的貨不滿意，您聲稱品質比原樣差，但這似乎不合理，因為我們在出貨前就有寄先行的樣品給你，而且並沒有從您那裡聽到和這相反的訊息。

因此我們認為這件事情（指出貨）是合乎規則的。

☉ 解說

1. You are not satisfied with the goods supplied to your order No. 123.：（您對我們供應給您第 123 號訂單的貨不滿意。）

   ＝ You are not satisfied with the goods which were supplied to your order No.123.

   本句省略 Which were 而成為分詞片語修飾 The goods。

2. Are not satisfied with：（對……不滿意）

   ┌─────○ 補充說明 ○─────┐

   限定修飾的形容詞子句中，若關係代名詞為主詞時，其所引導的形容詞子句可化簡為分詞片語（即現在分詞或過去分詞），方法如下：

   a. 去掉該關係代名詞。

   b. 把後面的動詞變成現在分詞。

   c. 若動詞為 Be 動詞，變成現在分詞 Being 省略。

   └─────────────────────┘

   例如：The baby who cried on bed is my son.

   去掉 Who → The baby crying on bed is my son.

   （在床上哭的嬰兒是我的兒子。）

I like the toys which are displayed in the shop window.

去掉 Which → I like the toys being displayed in the shop window.

再去掉 Being → I like the toys displayed in the shop window.

（我喜歡在商店櫥窗展示的那些玩具。）

3. Quality was inferior to the original sample：（品質比原樣差）

一般事物的比較級都用 Than。

例如：A is higher than B.（A 比 B 高）

C is larger than D.（C 比 D 大）

但 Inferior 要用 To，英文裡只有 2 個英文字，其比較級要用 To，一個是 Inferior，另一個是 Superior（較佳的、較好的）。

例如：A is inferior to B.（不可用 Than）

（A 比 B 差。）

B is superior to A.（不可用 Than）

（B 比 A 佳。）

4. Claim：此處的 Claim 不是索賠的意思是（聲稱）。

例如：He claimed that his answer was correct.

（他宣稱他的答案是正確的。）

5. Advance sample：（先行的樣品）

依客戶的原樣打造的樣品（Counter sample），先寄去給客戶確認，此樣品就是 Advance sample，這有別於 Keeping sample（留底樣品），這是生產後出貨時，從中取幾件留底的樣品。

6. Prior to：（在⋯⋯之前）＝ Before

7. To the contrary：（和這相反的）有相反的情形，通常放在句子後面。

例如：I will expect you on Friday unless I hear to the contrary.

（我期待您星期五來，除非我得到您相反的通知。）

Evidence to the contrary（相反的證據）

另外常見的 On the contrary（反之、相反地），等於

On the other hand，通常放在句子前面。

例如：I thought it was going to clear up. On the other hand, it began to rain.

（我原以爲天氣會放晴，相反地，天開始下雨了。）

8. Presume：（假定、推測）＝ Assume

例如：They presumed her to be dead.（他們推測她已死亡。）

They assumed him to be a complete stranger.

（他們以爲他是個完全陌生的人。）

We assumed that the train would be on time.

（我們以爲火車會準時。）

範例中 Presumed it to be in order.，省略主詞 We。

> ○ 補充說明 ○
>
> Assume、Presume、Suggest 等動詞組成的句子，前面主詞如果是第一人稱（I）或（We）時可以省略。

9. In order：（合乎規則的、適宜的）另 In order 也可做（安然）解釋，In good order ＝ Safely。

例如：The books arrived in good order.

（這些書安然無損地到達。）

▌範例三

（上文請參照範例二。）

This does not appear to be very reasonable as we have closely examined the sample taken from our last consignment and find it is no way different in quality. We can only surmise that there maybe a mistake somewhere.

翻譯

這似乎不合理，因我們已經仔細檢查過上次出貨的樣品，發現品質上根本沒有不同，我們只能猜想，或許在某方面有問題吧？

解說

1. Closely：（仔細地）＝ Carefully

2. The sample taken from our last consignment：
   ＝ The sample which was taken from our last consignment.
   省略關係代名詞及 Be 動詞，變成分詞片語。（其法則請參閱範例二中的補充說明。）

3. No way different：（沒有不同）＝ No different，Way 只是加強語氣而已。

4. We can only surmise that there maybe a mistake somewhere.：
   （我們只能猜想，大概在什麼地方出了差錯。）
   本句是給 Buyer 的下臺階，因為他說我們的品質不好，但我們檢查之後，並沒有發現品質有任何問題，那只好假設在某處出了問題，來化解僵局。（因有可能 Buyer 隨便找藉口要殺價或撈點利益，如果我們不據理力爭，可能會被得逞。）

5. Surmise：（推測）=Guess

例如：I surmised that his business had come to a stand stiff.

　　　（我猜想他的業務已經停頓。）

Surmise 與 Guess 的些許不同在於：

Surmise 是指憑直覺或想像來推測。

例如：We surmised her motive of suicide.

　　　（我們猜想她自殺的動機。）

而 Guess 是指對於不甚知道的事情，或憑不確實的證據，來判斷或估計。

例如：Guess the height of that hill.（猜猜這小丘的高度。）

▌範例四

You claimed the quality was inferior to the original sample.

After we made an examination we did not find any evidence of inferior quality or workmanship and the materials used were of the highest quality. We can only surmise that there maybe a mistake somewhere.

◎ 翻譯

　　您聲稱品質比原樣較差，但在我們檢查之後，並沒有發現有品質不良，或工藝不好的證據，而且所使用的原料，是最好的品質，因此我們猜想，可能在某處出了差錯吧！

◎ 解說

The materials used were of the highest quality：
（所使用的原料是最好的品質）

    a. Used 是 Use 的過去分詞，當形容詞使用，可放在被修飾的名詞 Materials 的前面或後面。

    b. Of the highest quality：（最好品質的、最高品質的）

        這個 Of 不可省略，因為 Quality 是抽象名詞，前面加上 Of，可當形容詞使用。

        例如：Judy is beauty.（Judy 是漂亮。）

            這是錯誤的，因為 Judy 是人，而 Beauty（漂亮）是抽象名詞，人當然不等於漂亮，我們只能說 Judy 是漂亮的，所以要寫成：

        Judy is of beauty.＝ Judy is beautiful.

        又如我們說「黃金很值錢」，不可以寫成 "Gold is value."
一定要寫成 "Gold is valuable." 或 "Gold is of value."。

        其他常見的還有 Of help ＝ helpful，Of use ＝ useful。

▌範例五

　　We have received your letter of July 15 and must apologize for sending you the goods of inferior quality. We have looked into the matter and find that your claim is perfectly justified. As suggested we agree to your selling the remainder of the goods at 20% below the list price.

◎ 翻譯

　　我們已收到貴方 7 月 15 日的來信，我們必須向您道歉，出了品質不良的貨給您，我們已調查這件事情，而且發現您的索賠是應該的。依照您的建議，我們同意您以低於定價的 20%，來銷售剩下的貨品。

◎ 解說

1. Look into：（調查）＝ Investigate
2. Justified：（證實為應該的），原形動詞 Justify（證明……為正當）。
3. Perfectly：（完美地）此處係加強語氣，強調 Buyer 的 Claim 是應該的，不必把 Perfectly 翻譯出來。

> ○──　補充說明　──○
>
> 客戶的 Claim 或 Complaint，如果調查之後，的確錯在我方，我們應該坦然承認，表示負責的態度。

4. Remainder：（剩餘之物或人）＝ The rest ＝ Balance，但

Balance 較常見於「帳戶」方面的差額。

例如：There is a balance in my favor of US$1,000.

　　　（我的帳上尚存美金 1,000 元。）

又如：The remainder of the goods will be shipped in the next few days.

　　　（剩餘貨物將在近日裝運。）

5. Agree to：（同意）這裡的 To 是介系詞，後面接事物的名詞等受詞，而 Agree with（同意）則用於對人或事。

例如：I agree with you.（我同意你。）

　　　I agree to your point.（我同意你的觀點。）

但當 Agree with 後面接事物時，大部分用在（與……相符）。

例如：We have to tell you that the goods sent by you do not agree with your sample.

　　　（我們必須告訴你，你出的貨品與你的樣品不符。）

Unit

6 特殊狀況的裝船通知

第一項　出貨時間緊迫以 **Back date** 方式裝船及押匯

▋ 範　例

Regret to inform you that shipment are unable to catch M/S "President" V-123 closing today because of unexpected traffic jam. We will ship on the next available vessel M/S "Taiwan" closing Keelung on Apr. 5.

As L/C stipulates "latest shipment date Mar. 30, 2022", please accept back-dated bill of lading showing "on board date" Mar. 30, 2022. So that we can negotiate documents with bank without discrepancy.

Please confirm by return.

翻譯

我們很遺憾通知您，貨物因預料不到的交通壅塞，來不及裝上今天結關的「總統輪」第 123 航次，我們會裝下一班 4 月 5 日在基隆結關的「臺灣輪」。

　　因為信用狀規定，最後裝船的日期是 2022 年 3 月 30 日，請接受我們倒填裝船日期的提單，上面記載「裝船日期」2022 年 3 月 30 日，以便我們可以向銀行押匯沒有瑕疵。

　　請馬上確認。

解說

1. Back date：（倒填裝船日期）

　　依照航政機關的規定，On board（裝船）的日期，要在貨物業已裝上船後才可登載，如果船方登載 On board date 比貨物裝運到船上的日期早，這叫 Back date，是違反規定的，所以一般船公司不輕易答應貨主的要求去做。

　　但國際貿易實務上，買賣雙方因不願多花 Amend L/C 的費用，而直接要求船方做 Back date，以符合 L/C 的要求，或者賣方因趕工不及，導致裝船日超過 L/C 規定的日期，所以偷偷地要求船方配合做 Back date。（不讓 Buyer 知道，是怕 Buyer 會藉機殺價或 Complain。）

2. Please accept back-dated bill of lading showing "on board date" Mar. 30, 2022.（請接受登載「裝船日期」2022 年 3 月 30 日的倒填日期提單。）

　　＝ Please accept back-dated bill of lading which shows "on board date" Mar. 30, 2022.

2-1. Showing 前面省略關係代名詞 Which，而簡化成分詞片語。（其法則請參閱單元三中的第三項範例解說。）

2-2. Back-dated：（倒填裝船日期的）是 Back date 的過去分詞，當形容詞使用，修飾 Bill of lading。

第二項 改走空運

依 Buyer 要求改走空運。

■ 範　例

　　We acknowledge receipt of your confirmation that your consignment should be sent by air-freight, and we have accordingly forwarded the goods.　We trust that the consignment arrives safely.　We have enclosed a copy of the Air Waybill in this letter for your reference.

翻譯

　　我們已收到您的確認，說您的貨物要走空運，我們也已依照規定出了貨，相信這批貨會安然到達，隨函附上空運提單複本供參照。

解說

By air-freight：（走空運）慣稱 By air-cargo，有時簡寫 By air，走海運簡寫 By sea。

a.　Freight 有兩種意思，一為（貨物）、另一為（運價），為了避免混淆，船公司或航空公司通常會把運價寫成 Freight charges，費率寫成 Freight rates。

b.　在運輸界來講 Freight ＝ Cargo ＝ Shipment ＝ Consignment。

第三項　遇到船公司轉船時

當遇到船公司轉船時，建議 Buyer 改走空運。

▌ 範　例

　　As you need the goods urgently we suggest part of the goods be sent by air.　You can expect the cargo (consignment) in next 3 days.

翻譯

　　因您急需這批貨，我們建議部分的貨走空運，您可以預期在 3 天內收到這些空運的貨。

解說

We suggest part of the goods be sent by air.：

＝ We suggest to you that part of the goods should be sent by air.

（我們建議您部分的貨走空運。）

省略 To you（向您）及 Should（應該），所以 Be 動詞用原式。

例如：I suggested (to him) that the sum (should) be paid immediately.

　　　（我向他提議立刻付款。）

○ 補充說明 ○

a. Should 的省略多見於美國

　　例如：I suggested that he (should) leave the room.

　　　　（我建議他應離開房間。）

○ 補充說明 ○

b. 另外

Propose

Recommend

Require　　　＋ That 使用到 Should 時，Should 可
　　　　　　以省略。
Request

Insist　　　　例如：He proposed that we (should)

Order　　　　　　lower the price.

　　　　　　（他提議我們應該降價。）

第四項　遇到出貨 Delay，客戶又急著要貨時

遇到出貨 Delay，客戶又急著要貨時，可以建議客戶一半的貨走空運，一半的貨走海運，避免全部走空運以減少運送成本。（或全部使用海空聯運。）

▌範　例

Our cargo was left behind because of the operation carelessness of the forwarding agent. As requested we will send half of the goods by air at our expense and the rest by next available vessel.（Or all the cargo will be shipped via Sea-Air transport service.）

翻譯

　　由於承運的代理商作業上的疏失，導致我們的貨被擱置而無法運出，依照您的要求我們會把一半的貨走空運，運費由我方負擔，剩下的貨走下班船。（或全部的貨使用海空聯運來運送。）

解說

1. Was left behind：（被留置）有時因船公司 OP 人員作業上的疏失，例如：配櫃方面裝不下，而需走下班船等。
2. At our expense：（由我方付費）＝ For our account
3. The rest：（剩餘之物或人）＝ Remainder

第五項　遇到船公司在新加坡或香港轉船時

範　例

　　Our cargo was unloaded at Singapore by the carrier who made transhipment there due to operation reason. We have urged shipping agent to reload our goods and forward by first available vessel.

翻譯

　　我們的貨因作業上需轉船，被運送人卸在新加坡等待轉運，我們已敦促船運代理商，儘速把貨再裝上下一班船運出。

⊚ 解說

1. Carrier：（運送人）

    運送人有二種，一是擁有運輸工具從事實際運送業務之業者，如船公司、航空公司。另一種是不擁有運輸工具，但承擔執行運送業務之業者，例如：NVOCC（Non-vessel own/operating common carrier）。目前我們臺灣的 Freight forwarder（貨運承攬商），都是屬於這種性質的承攬運送人。

2. Transhipment：（轉船、轉運）

    根據 UCP 600（信用狀統一慣例）的說明，所謂 transhipment，就是由 A 船把貨卸下（Unload），然後再把此貨物重裝（Reload）到 B 船。最明顯的例子是子船接母船，這就發生轉船（運）的問題，但 UCP 600 有解釋，只要貨物是裝在貨櫃中，從啟運地到目的地，只有一套提單涵蓋整個運送過程，縱使 L/C 規定不可轉船，押匯時銀行不會認為有瑕疵。

    這條有關於轉船的規定主要是針對散裝貨（Break-bulk cargo），亦即不是裝在貨櫃的貨物（Container cargo），因散裝貨轉船時容易損壞之故。

Unit 7 三角貿易

第一項 船期的安排

對三角貿易來講，Buyer 並不反對 Supplier 在何處生產或製造，只要品質及價錢可以接受的話，但對於遠在第三國生產，如何控制出貨、安排船期，倒是有疑慮，如果我們要用英文向 Buyer 來敘述出貨問題，未免太複雜又浪費時間。在此我們試舉一例，說明臺灣接單，廈門生產，貨要出到德國漢堡。

用下列方式表達比較簡單明瞭，如有必要時再以備註方式，加以補充說明即可。

■ 範 例

Re：Shipping arrangement for your order No. 123

Feeder VSL	Voyage	Xiamen close	ETD	ETA H.K.	Mother VSL	Voyage	ETD H.K.	ETA HAM
King	123	4/15	4/16	4/17	Queen	456	4/19	5/15

Remarks: For your information it will take more time to transport the goods from Xiamen to H.K. by truck. Besides, the inland truckage is more expensive.

⊚ 翻譯

主旨：您的訂單第 123 號船期的安排

子船	航次	廈門結關	預計開航時間	預計到達時間	母船	航次	香港結關	預計到達時間
King	123	4/15	4/16	4/17	Queen	456	4/19	5/15

備註：請知悉，從廈門到香港用卡車運送貨物，將比較花費時間，而且內陸卡車費也比較貴。

⊚ 解說

1. Feeder vessel：（子船或稱支線集貨船）VSL 是 Vessel 的縮寫。跑近海的船隻，載運量較小，大概 1,000TEU 以下，被用來作為母船運送貨櫃的交通船，這樣會比母船彎靠每一港口裝卸貨，來得經濟、方便。

2. ETA：Estimated time of arrival（預計船抵達的時間）
   ETD：Estimated time of departure（預計船開航的時間）
   由於天候、風浪等因素，均足以影響船、飛機速度，因此無法預先公布準確的抵達或開航的日期時間，以免引發糾紛。

第二項　單據文件配合問題

　　如果 Buyer 為了某種原因，尤其是想規避配額問題，要您修改提單上的裝貨港時，您可以婉拒此要求，因為這是違法的，船公司不會接受，主要是由於海運提單係屬有價證券，做不實的登載，例如：提單做 Back date 或更改裝貨港口，將構成偽造有價證券，處罰是很重的。

> ▌ 範例一

So far as shipping documents are concerned the port of loading in the B/L will be issued as Hong Kong if shipment is made at Hong Kong. And shipping Co., will not change it to Keelung as loading port because it is illegal.

翻譯

　　有關裝船文件，提單上的裝貨港將被作成香港，如果貨物是從香港裝運，而且船公司是不會把它改作成基隆港的，因為那是違法的。

解說

1. Illegal：（違法的）＝ Unlawful
   Legal 指較狹義的合法，亦即合乎法律條文。
   Lawful 指較廣義的合法，亦即指合乎法律精神。
   例如：A legal profession（合法的職業）
   　　　A lawful business（合法的事業）
2. Issue：（開出、發行、簽發）

■ 範例二

When you have the L/C opened, please stipulate shipment to be made from any Chinese port instead of Hong Kong. So that we can ship the goods direct from any main port in China nearest to our factory. By doing so, we do not have to ship the goods to Hamburg in transhipment at Hong Kong. Meantime, we can negotiate documents with bank without discrepancy.

翻譯

當您開立信用狀時,請規定出貨是從任何中國的港口,而不是香港,這樣我們就可以從距離工廠最近的中國主要港口,把貨裝運出去,而不必經由香港轉運到漢堡,同時我們押匯時也不會有瑕疵。

第三項 交貨條件的選擇(FOB 或 CFR)

由於三角貿易貨物是由境外裝運,比較不容易控制,因此最好是由工廠自己找船,自己付運費,亦即交貨條件採用 CFR 或 CIF,只要工廠的價格我們能接受,同時嚴格規定交貨的日期,那麼我們就不必去擔憂種種出貨的事情了,諸如空櫃、報關、艙位等問題,但我們必須說服 Buyer,把交貨條件 FOB 改 CFR/CIF。其範例如下:

▌範 例

With regard to shipment we have no objection to FOB terms from H.K. and will comply with your instructions. But one thing we would like to point out that the peak delivery season will start from July and the shipping space will become very tight. We are afraid our supplier may not obtain needed space from NYK.

In view of our long established business relation with Maersk, we are assured of protection of space for our cargo from Xiamen to Hamburg. Please consider this matter and change the shipment terms to CIF Hamburg by Maersk if possible.

翻譯

關於出貨，我們不反對從香港裝運的 FOB 條件，而且我們會遵照您的指示，不過有一件事情我們想提出來，那就是出貨旺季即將從 7 月分開始，艙位會變得很緊，我們擔心我們的供應廠商可能無法從 NYK 船公司訂到所需要的艙位。

由於我們與 Maersk 船公司，有長久建立的商業關係，我們被保證，貨物從廈門到漢堡的艙位可以得到保障，請您考慮這一件事情，如有可能請把交貨條件改為 CIF，並使用 Maersk 的船。

🎯 解說

1. No objection to：（對……不反對）

   Objection to（反對）＝ Oppose 或 Be opposed to（反對……），這些 To 都是介系詞，所以後面要接名詞等受詞，而 Oppose 後面，可以直接接反對的事物。

2. From H.K.：也可以寫成 Ex H.K.，Ex 是介系詞（自……）＝ From。

   商業英文中，Ex 通常指 From 之意。而一般的用語中，Ex 通常指（以前的、在前的）＝ Former，如 Ex-wife（前妻）、Ex-president（前總統）。

   請注意 Late president 則是（已故總統），Late wife 則是（亡妻）。

3. Point out：（指出）

4. Peak delivery season：（出貨旺季）Peak 是名詞（最高點、頂點）。

   例如：The peak of traffic（最大的交通量）

5. Long established：（長期已建立的）Established 是過去分詞當形容詞使用，修飾 Business relation（商業關係）。

6. If possible：（如有可能、可能的話）徵詢對方，希望對方同意的客氣用法。

Unit 8 出貨後的後遺症問題及因應之道

 說 明

　　出貨後裝了船，拿了提單押匯，這並不代表此一訂單的外銷工作已結束，它只是暫告一段落罷了，因為有可能會發生下列情形。

第一項　Consignee 遲不提貨

範　例

　　We are informed by shipping company that so far you have not taken delivery of the consignment.　We would remind you customs regulations require that consignee complete customs clearance procedures within 15 days of the arrival of the vessel.　Otherwise, overtime charge will be levied up to a limit of 30 days.　If the delivery of the cargo is not taken at the end of the 30 days it may be auctioned.

⊚ 翻譯

　　我們被船公司告知，到目前為止，您尚未去提貨，我們想提醒您，海關規則規定，在船到 15 天內，受貨人必須完成清關手續，否則要被徵收滯報費直到 30 天為止，如果 30 天到了還沒辦理提貨的話，這批貨就可能遭海關拍賣。

⊚ 解說

1. Take delivery：（提貨）＝ Take delivery of the consignment（提領交運中的貨物）

2. Customs regulations：（海關規則）

3. Customs clearance procedures：（海關通關手續）
   Complete customs clearance procedures（清關）＝ Clear customs（用在口語化或簡化）

4. Overtime charge：（滯報費）
   海關規定船到港後，貨主須在 15 天內辦理報關提貨，否則要罰滯報費，例如：每天 NT$20 元。

5. Levied：原形動詞 Levy（徵收），僅用於政府有關的稅收的徵收，如所得稅、貨物稅、關稅等。
   Collect 也可做徵收用，但範圍較大，不只限於政府方面的稅收，例如：收取款項、募集資金等。

6. A limit of 30 days：（30 天的限制）亦即以 30 天為限。

7. It may be auctioned：（它可能被拍賣）It 指這批貨。

第二項　信用狀被止付（Unpaid）

■ 範　例

We are surprised to receive a notice from our bankers here that the draft for US$5,000 drawn on ABC bank under L/C No.567 covering your order No.123 has been dishonored (unpaid).

Our negotiation bank told us it was due to absence of documents called for under the credit. As the said draft has already negotiated and we are in a very embarrassing situation. We will send the required documents as soon as they are available.

翻譯

我們很驚訝接到我們這裡的銀行的通知說，我們所開立以 ABC 銀行為付款人的匯票，美金 5,000 元已遭止付，此匯票是根據第 567 號信用狀，涵蓋您的第 123 號訂單。

押匯銀行告訴我們，這是因為欠缺信用狀所要求的文件所致，由於我們業已押匯，處境困窘，請跟貴方銀行安排立刻付款，一旦所需的文件準備好了，我們會馬上寄出。

解說

1. Bankers：（銀行業者）＝ Bank
2. The draft for US$5,000 drawn on ABC bank under L/C No.567 covering your order No.123 has been dishonored：

（以 ABC 銀行為付款人，所開立的匯票美金 5,000 元，已遭止付，此匯票是根據第 567 號信用狀，涵蓋您第 123 號的訂單）

2-1.　The draft 是 That 子句中的主詞，動詞是 Has been dishonored（或 Unpaid），其餘 Draft 後面的 "For US$5,000 drawn on ABC bank under L/C No.567 covering your order No.123" 都是在修飾 Draft。一個長句子只要先找出主詞及動詞，那麼其意思就已明朗。

2-2.　Drawn on：（以……為付款人）匯票開給誰，他就是付款人，亦即 Drawee（被出票人）。

　　　　Draw 是（開立）＝ Issue。例如：Draw a check（開支票）。

　　　　Draw a draft（開匯票），被動語態為 A draft is drawn。

　　　　Drawn on 則是匯票被開給某人，他就是被出票人，英文是 Drawee，出票人英文是 Drawer，通常是出口商。

　　　◦補充說明◦

　　　在信用狀的交易，匯票的 Drawee 通常是開狀銀行或付款銀行，但在 D/A 及 D/P 的付款條件下，Drawee 被出票人，則是進口商本身，也就是付款人。

2-3.　Under L/C No.567 covering your order No.123：

　　　　Under 在此處應解釋為（根據）。

　　　　Covering 是（涵蓋），前面省略關係代名詞 Which 而成為分詞片語，用來修飾前面的前述詞 L/C No.567。

　　　　本句等於 Under L/C No.567 which covers your order No.123.

3.　Absence of documents called for under the credit：

　　（根據信用狀所要求的文件不齊全）

＝ Absence of documents which were called for under the credit.

Called for（要求），前面省略關係代名詞 Which Were 而成爲分詞片語，修飾 Documents。

4. The said：（上述的）＝ The above mentioned

第三項　退運問題

當我們所出的貨，品質不良或 Item 搞錯，Buyer 堅持要退回時。

┃ 範　例

* We will arrange forwarding agent to collect the goods and send back to Taiwan. Please give necessary assistance to them.
* Please arrange to have the goods sent back to us on freight collect basis.

◎ 翻譯

* 我們將安排承運的代理商到貴處收貨並送回臺灣，請給予必要的協助。
* 請安排把貨運回給我們，運費以到付方式處理。

◎ 解說

1. To have the goods sent back to us：（請把貨物運回給我們），其句構如同單元一第一種理由的範例解說中第 7 點 To have the L/C opened（請開立信用狀）的用法一樣。

2. On freight collect basis：（運費以到付爲準）

On...basis 是以……爲條件，或以……爲基礎，例如：On FOB basis（以 FOB 交貨條件爲準）。

第四項　**正本提單遺失急著提貨問題**

▌ 範　例

After tracing so far we still do not know whereabouts of the shipping documents. In order to take delivery of consignment timely, please approach the carrier and arrange the delivery by "Indemnity and guarantee delivery without Bill of Lading."

翻譯

在我們追蹤之後，到目前爲止，我們還是不知道這些裝船文件的下落，爲了要適時地提貨，請與運送人接洽，並安排「擔保提貨」。

解說

1. Take delivery：（提貨）＝ Take delivery of consignment
2. Whereabouts：（在哪裡）
3. Timely：（適時地）＝ In due course，注意 In time 是（及時），而 On time 是（準時），都與 Timely 的意思不同。
4. Approach：（接洽、交涉）＝ Contact

5. Indemnity and guarantee delivery without Bill of Lading.：

（擔保提貨不用出示提單。）

由於正本提單遺失，受貨人無法依正常程序提貨，而向運送人申請擔保提貨，請開狀銀行背書保證，運送人就根據此擔保提貨申請書放貨，日後如開狀銀行收到提單時，再向運送人換回此申請書。

> ○ 補充說明 ○
>
> 擔保提貨與副提單背書提貨不同，副提單背書提貨英文為 Delivery against duplicate bill of lading endorsed by banker。

係進口商於申請開發 L/C 時，在信用狀中規定，出口商出貨後，將一份正本提單，直接寄給進口商，這一份正本提單稱為副提單（Duplicate B/L），進口商憑此副提單，向開狀銀行請求背書，以便辦理報關提貨，其餘的正本提單（通常是二份），由出口商持向押匯銀行辦理押匯。對船公司而言，進口商憑此副提單提貨後，其餘二份正本提單即自動失效。

6. Surrender：（交出）＝ Present

例如：Surrender the bill of lading（交出提單）

Unit 9 催促付款（L/C Payment 之外）

🔒 說明

　　與客戶往來久了以後，雙方已建立互信的基礎，對於付款方式逐漸不用 L/C，以節省信用狀交易所產生的種種費用，如開發費、修改費、瑕疵費等，但其他的付款方式諸如 T.T.（Telegraphic transfer）、D/A（Documents against acceptance）、D/P（Documents against payments）等，則有可能發生 Buyer 延後付款或賴帳等情事，對於處理這些情況的英文寫法如下。

▌範例一

　　We have rendered our April statement of account twice and regret that the amount of US$5,000 is still outstanding. We should be grateful for an early settlement.

🎯 翻譯

　　我們已經給您四月分的帳單明細表二次了，但遺憾的是，這美金 5,000 元的款項迄今未付，我們將感謝早日付款。

◎ 解說

1. Render：（提供、給予）

    例如：What service did he render to you?

    （他給予您什麼服務？）

2. Statement of account：（帳目報告表）俗稱帳單明細表。

    此係將有關同一客戶的應收、應付金額予以加減，並將各借項清單（Debit note）及貸項清單（Credit note）的明細予以摘錄，作成帳目明細表，以說明該金額的由來，然後寄給對方請其清償。

3. Outstanding：債務等（未付的）

4. Settlement：（付款、解決）＝ Payment

▌範例二

　　We wish to draw your attention to our invoice No.123 for the sum of US$5,000 which is still unpaid.

　　As the amount is now more than a month overdue, we trust you will settle it within the next few days.

◎ 翻譯

　　我們想提醒您注意，我們第 123 號金額 5,000 元的發票，迄今未付。

　　因為此款項已過期一個月，我們相信您會在這幾天之內付款。

◎ 解說

1.　We wish to：Wish 與 Hope 皆可做完全及物動詞，以不定詞做
　　受詞。

　　例如：I wish to do it.（我希望做此事。）

　　　　　＝ I hope to do it.

　　但 Hope 不能做不完全及物動詞，不可接受詞及不定詞做受詞
　　補語。

　　例如：I hope him to do it.（我希望他去做此事。）是錯誤的，
　　應改為 I wish him to do it.

2.　Draw your attention to：（提醒您注意……）

　　　＝ Bring your attention to...

3.　Overdue：（過期的、遲到的）

　　例如：The train is overdue.（火車誤點了。）

■ 範例三

　　We are enclosing a statement of your account up to
and including June 30 showing a balance in our favor of
US$1,000 which we hope you will find in order (correct).

　　We look forward to your remittance by return.

◎ 翻譯

　　我們隨函檢附您的帳單，此帳單是到 6 月 30 日這天（含）
為止，我們有盈餘 1,000 美金，希望您會發現此金額是正確
的，我們期待您立刻匯款。

解說

1. Including：（包括、含）原形動詞 Include 的現在分詞，修飾 A statement of your account，是由省略關係代名詞 Which 而變成的句構。

2. In order：（正確的）＝ Correct，作為 Which 的受詞補語，而 Which 是不完全及物動詞 Find 的受詞。

範例四

　　We regret not having received a reply to our letter of May 10, 2022 reminding you that your account had not been settled.

　　Please let us know immediately when we may expect the settlement of your outstanding account.

翻譯

　　我們很遺憾，還沒有接到您對我們 2022 年 5 月 10 日寫給您的信的回覆，那封信是在提醒您，您的帳單還沒有付款。

　　請立刻讓我們知道，何時我們可以接到您未付帳單的款項。

解說

1. Regret：（遺憾）可做動詞或名詞使用，請注意下列用法。
   Regret ＋動名詞：（後悔曾、遺憾曾）事情已經發生。
   Regret ＋ to ＋動詞：（抱歉要、遺憾要）事情將要發生。

例如：I regret telling you the truth.（我後悔曾告訴您真相。）

意謂已經講出真相。

I regret to tell you the truth.（我抱歉要告訴您真相。）

意謂還沒有說出真相，正要說出來。

其他如：I forgot to see him.（我忘了要去看他。）

I forget seeing him before.（我忘了曾經見過他。）

2. Reply：（答覆）＝ Answer，皆可做動詞或名詞使用，但做動詞時，Reply 後面要加介系詞 To，Answer 則不用。

例如：Answer my question ＝ Reply to my question

○── 補充說明 ──○

Answer 表示以口頭、筆寫或行動回答之意，屬最普通的用語。Reply 則用於較正式的文體中，表示經過較仔細考慮後的答覆。

▌ 範例五

We notice that your account which was due for payment on April 30, 2022 still remains unpaid.

We must now ask you to settle this account by return.

◎ 翻譯

我們注意到，您應在 2022 年 4 月 30 日到期的帳單，依然未付。

我們現在必須要求您立刻付清此帳單。

解說

1. Due：（應到期的）

   例如：The check is due on the 15th of May.

   （這張支票在 5 月 15 日到期。）

2. Remain：（依然是）

   Appear、Seem、Become、Remain 等動詞之後接分詞作爲主詞補語，而做主詞補語的分詞均爲形容詞。

   例如：The natural beauty of the country remains unchanged.

   （這國家的天然美景依然是不變的。）

   Unchanged 是過去分詞當形容詞使用，做主詞補語。

   又如：Judy became interested in playing piano.

   （Judy 對彈鋼琴有興趣了。）

   He seems tired.

   （他似乎累了。）

3. Must ask you：（必須要求您）

   比 Would ask you 及 Ask you 更爲強烈。

4　By return：（立刻）＝ Soon ＝ Immediately

Unit 10 不同意延期付款

🔒 **說 明**

　　經過多次催款無效，想賴帳的客戶經常會藉故要求延付，對於這種 Buyer，我們應付的英文如下。

■ **範 例**

　　We have carefully considered the proposal in your letter of April 30, while sympathizing with you for the loss and inconvenience caused by the fire which occurred at your warehouse.

　　We understand your current standing. However, we are unable to overlook the fact that your payments have been delayed so frequently.

　　Please try to understand that we also have our obligations. Therefore we must ask you to arrange to make payment at once. Otherwise, we shall be forced to take the legal action.

翻譯

　　我們已經很仔細地考慮到您 4 月 30 日信上的建議，同時同情您因為倉庫火災產生的損失及不便。

　　我們瞭解您現在的處境，但我們不能忽視您對於付款經常延誤。

　　請您也要瞭解我們也有負擔，因此我們必須要求您立刻安排付款，否則我們將被迫採取法律行動。

解說

1. While sympathizing with you for the loss...：

　　（正當我們同情您……）省略主詞及 Be 動詞。

　　＝ While we are sympathizing with you for the loss...

補充說明

Once、When、While、If、Unless、Though 等六個連接詞，所引導的副詞子句中，若主詞與主句中的主詞相同時，可以將此副詞子句，化簡為分詞句構，其法則如下：

a. 將主詞省略。

b. 動詞改為分詞。

c. 動詞如果是 Be 動詞，改為分詞後可以省略。

例如：While she was walking along the street, she met Mr. White.

　　　（當她在街上走著的時候，她遇到懷特先生。）

　　　＝ While walking along the street, she met Mr. White.

又如：If I am free, I will go with you.

　　　（如果我有空，我會跟您去。）

　　　　　＝ If free, I will go with you.

2. Sympathize：（同情）

　　 Sympathize with ＋人＋ for ＋事情

　　 同情某人介系詞用 With，同情某事用 For。

3. Current：（現今的、現時的）

　　 例如：The current situation（現在的情況）

4. Stand：（處境）名詞是 Standing。

　　 例如：Peter stands in danger.（Peter 處境危險。）

5. How you now stand：（您目前處境如何）

6. Frequently：（經常）＝ Often

7. Obligations：（職責、負擔）

8. Take the legal action：（採取法律行動）亦即向法院提出訴訟。

Unit

11　Debit Note/ Credit Note 的用法

🔒 說 明

　　在國際貿易的過程中，難免會有小金額往來的交易，例如：樣品費、代墊款、郵寄費用等，如果每筆小金額的交易，幾百美元甚或幾十美元，都要寫信催款，逐筆匯款或寄支票，實在浪費時間又不好看，尤其是母公司與子公司之間、總代理與經銷商之間，更沒有必要逐筆結帳。

　　這種小金額的交易，最好是採取記帳的方式，雙方約定一個月結一次，或三個月結一次。如果往來次數頻繁交易筆數多，則每月結清，否則三個月甚至半年結一次都可以，反正金額也不大。

　　所謂記帳，就是在公司的帳目中設立對方的帳戶，用借方代付款（Debit）及貸方代收款（Credit），分別登載應收帳款及應付帳款，到結帳日時兩者相抵。假如甲公司帳戶的借方有餘額，表示甲公司積欠我們，這時我們要寄 Debit Note 給對方，向其要錢；如果是甲公司的帳戶，出現貸方有餘額，表示我們積欠甲公司錢，這時我們就要寄 Credit Note 給對方，向其表示我們欠他們多少錢，最好連同支票一起寄給甲公司，以結清這段期間的帳款。

　　這種不需以文辭來表達催錢、欠錢的方式，不失為比較婉轉客氣的用法。

例如：

ABC 公司

借　方		貸　方	
1/5 樣品費	$100	1/10 關稅代墊款	$200
1/5 郵費	$50	1/20 索賠	$100
1/10 保險費	$50	1/30 佣金	$100
1/30 總計：	$200		$400
		貸方盈餘	$200

ABC CO., LTD

Debit		Credit	
1/5 Sample	$100	1/10 Duties Advanced	$200
1/5 Postage	$50	1/20 Claim	$100
1/10 Premium	$50	1/30 Commission	$100
1/30 Total：	$200		$400
		Balance	$200

第一項　**Debit Note**

　　人家欠我們錢，我們寄 Debit Note 給他，對方就知道我們在向他們催錢。

▍範　例

Debit Note	
To: ABC Co., Ltd.	Date: _____
	No.: _____
Descriptions	Amount
1. Sample charges	US$100.00
2. Postage	50.00
3. Premium	50.00
	US$200.00
XYZ Ent. Co., Ltd.	
_____	
Manager	

⌖ 解說

Debit Note：（借項通知單）俗稱帳單，人家寄 Debit Note 給您，就表示要您還錢付款之意。

> ○ 補充說明 ○
>
> 人家欠我們錢，我們寄 Debit Note 給對方，等對方寄來支票，我們收到時，要寫簡函通知對方已收到並致謝。

例如：

We were pleased to receive your bank cheque for US$1,000. It has been credited to your statement of account which is now completely clear. Please give us the opportunity to serve you again.

（我們很高興接到您的銀行支票美金 1,000 元，我們已把它列入您明細表帳戶中的貸方，此帳戶現已完全結清，希望能有再次為您服務的機會。）

第二項　Credit Note

　　我們欠人家錢，為表示誠意，寄 Credit Note 給對方，改天再寄支票或匯款，以結清此段期間的帳款。

■ 範　例

Credit Note	
To: XYZ Ent. Co., Ltd.	Date: _____
	No.: _____
Descriptions	Amount
1. Duties advanced	US$200.00
2. Claim	100.00
3. Commission	100.00
ABC Co., Ltd.	US$400.00
_____	
Manager	

◎ 解說

Credit Note：（貸項通知單）俗稱折讓單。

Unit

12　與船務有關的 L/C 疑難辭句

■ 範例一

　　Bills of Lading must evidence carrying steamer is not registered in Israel or owned by nationals or residents of Israel and will not call at, or pass through any Israeli port enroute to Saudi Arabia. Also declaring that the said vessel is otherwise eligible to enter into the ports of the Kingdom of Saudi Arabia in conformity with its laws and regulations. Alternatively, declaration to this effect showing name, nationality and owner of vessel, appended to the Bills of Lading signed by owners or agents of vessel is acceptable and must accompany the documents.

◎ 翻譯

　　提單必須證明，所裝運的船隻不在以色列註冊，或不被以色列的國民或居民所擁有，而且此船隻，在前往沙烏地阿拉伯途中，將不彎靠或經過任何以色列的港口，同時提單要聲明，上述的船隻是被允許可以進入沙烏地阿拉伯王國的港口，並遵守其法律及規定。

或者，提出具有此同等效力的聲明書，由船舶的船東或代理簽字，上面登載船名、國籍及船東，附在提單上，亦可被接受，而且必須跟隨裝船單據。

解說

1. National：（國民）常用複數。

2. Resident：（居民）Residents 與 Nationals 不同在於居民不一定擁有國籍，但有居留權，而國民則是擁有國籍的。

3. Call at：（彎靠、停靠）不論大小港口，一律用介系詞 At，不能用 In。

4. Enroute to：（到……途中），類似 On the way to...。

5. Otherwise：（在其他方面）副詞，修飾 Eligible（有資格的），此處的 Otherwise 不能解釋為（否則、要不然）。所以本句 The said vessel is otherwise eligible to enter... 翻譯成：上述的船隻在其他方面是有資格進入……，亦即被允許可以進入……。

6. In conformity with：（遵守）

7. Alternatively：（二者取其一地）即二擇一之意，本文中，如果不在提單上證明……，就要提出一份聲明書來證明……。

8. Declaration to this effect showing... and must accompany the documents.：
這一句很長，要瞭解其意思，一定要先找出主詞及動詞，主詞是 Declaration to this effect（對這種效力的聲明書），其後的 Showing name, Nationality and owner of vessel, Appended to the Bills of Lading 及 Signed by owners or agents of vessel 都是分詞片語，都在修飾前面的主詞 Declaration to this effect，動

詞則是 Be 動詞 Is Acceptable（是可以被接受的）。Acceptable 是形容詞做主詞的補語。

9. And must accompany the documents：（而且必須跟隨裝船單據）＝ And declaration to this effect must accompany the documents. 因與 Is acceptable 的主詞相同，所以此處的主詞可以省略。The documents 指的是 Shipping documents（裝船文件）。

◦ 補充說明 ◦

範例一就是要求所謂的「黑名單證明書」（Blacklist certificate），阿拉伯國家所開出的信用狀上，通常要求出口商提示船公司黑名單證明書，證明該船隻未被列入阿拉伯國家的黑名單，而且保證駛往阿拉伯的航行途中，絕不彎靠或經過以色列的任何港口。

▌範例二

　　B/L must certify that the carrying steamer is not over 15 years of age at the time of loading.　Otherwise the vessel must have a valid certificates for cargo gear and tackle issued by one of the following societies approved by the government of Saudi Arabia, and copy of the same must accompany the documents.

翻譯

提單必須證明所裝貨的船隻，在裝貨時的船齡不超過 15 年，否則的話，這艘船必須有一張裝貨機具有效的證明書，此證明書是由沙烏地阿拉伯政府所核准的下列團體之一所簽發，而且證明書的影本必須跟隨著單據。

解說

1. Cargo gear and tackle：（裝貨的機具）指船上的吊桿等裝貨機器設備。

2. Society：（協會、公會、團體）

3. Otherwise the vessel must have a valid certificates...by the government of Saudi Arabia：

   這一句很長，先找出主詞及動詞，主詞是 The vessel，動詞是 Must have，其受詞是 A valid certificates for cargo gear and tackle（一張有效的裝貨機具證明書），其後的 Issued by one of the following societies approved by the government of Saudi Arabia，是分詞片語，修飾前面的受詞 A valid certificate。Approved 前面省略關係代名詞 Which were，而成為分詞片語用來修飾 Societies。

4. Same：代名詞（同一件事物）常作 The same。

   例如：He called for the same again.（他再要求相同的東西。）

   本文中 Same 代替 Certificates 避免重複同樣的字眼。

█ 範例三

Marine insurance policy or certificate for CIF value plus 10% covering Institute Cargo Clauses (All Risks), Institute War Clauses and Institute Strikes Riots and Civil Commotions Clauses.

◎ 翻譯

　　貨物海運保單或證明單，其保險金額是 CIF 的總值加上 10%，承保協會貨物保險的 A 條款（全險），及協會附加險的兵險及罷工、暴動、內亂險。

◎ 解說

1. Marine insurance policy or certificate：

　Insurance policy：（保險單）簡稱保單，係證明保險人與被保險人之間，成立保險契約的正式文件，載明雙方當事人所約定的權利、義務。

　而 Insurance certificate 是（保險證明書），係在保險人與被保險人之間，訂有 Open policy（預約保險契約）時，當貨主（被保險人）向保險公司（保險人）通報每批貨物的裝運資料時，由保險公司所開立，證明貨物已由某一 Open policy 承保的證明書。

　由於 Insurance policy 與 Insurance certificate 具有相同的效力，因此 L/C 上大都規定 "Insurance policy or certificate"，只要受益人提出任何一種，均可被接受。

○── 補充說明 ──○

Open policy（預約保單）這是由保險公司（保險人）承保貨主（被保險人），在某一定期間如一年或半年內，所有須由被保險人負擔運輸保險的貨物，全部交由該預約保險人承保，而由保險公司所簽發的一項總括性保險契約，貨主只要在每一批貨物裝運確定時，將保險金額、貨物名稱、數量、船名、起運日期及起訖地點，向保險公司聲明，即完成手續。

2. Institute cargo clauses：（協會貨物保險）的基本險，有 A 條款即慣稱的全險，B 條款類似以前舊的水漬險，及 C 條款類似以前舊的平安險。

■ 範例四

This credit is subject to Uniform Customs and Practice for Documentary Credits (2007 Revision) International Chamber of Commerce, publication No. 600.

◎ 翻譯及解說

請參見單元二中第一種藉口的範例補充說明 5-1。

▌範例五

　　Insurance policies or certificates in assignable form, and endorsed in blank for 10% above invoice value with claims payable in Hong Kong in currency of draft covering Institute Cargo Clauses (All Risks) and Institute War Clauses & S.R.C.C. & TPND.

◎ 翻譯

　　保險單或證明書，要為可以轉讓的型式，而且要在空白處背書，其金額為高於發票總值的一成，索賠的賠償地點在香港，賠償幣別與匯票同，保險涵蓋協會貨物保險的基本險Ａ條款（即全險），及附加險中的兵險及罷工、暴動、內亂險，還有竊盜遺失險。

◎ 解說

1. Assignable：（可讓渡的）
2. Endorsed in blank：（在空白處背書）
3. Payable：（應付的）例如：Freight payable at destination（運費應在目的地支付）
4. In currency of draft：（以匯票的貨幣），Currency 是（貨幣、通貨）。
5. 本句中 In assignable form、Endorsed in blank、For 10% above invoice value、With claims payable in Hong Kong、In currency of draft 及 Covering institute cargo... 都是片語（有介系詞片語、

分詞片語），都在修飾 Insurance policies or certificates。

█ 範例六

Signed commercial invoice, 5-fold, bearing seller's declaration that the country of origin is not marked on goods, their polybags or the inner cartons if any.

◎ 翻譯

有適當簽名的商業發票五份，登載賣方的聲明，說明原產國不會被標示在產品上、產品的包裝塑膠袋上，或內盒上如果有的話。

◎ 解說

1. 5-Fold：即五份的意思，等於 5 Copies，也等於 Quintuplicate。
   單據份數表示的方式有三種：
   1 Copy ＝ 1 Fold ＝ Original 一份（指正本）
   2 Copies ＝ 2 Folds ＝ Duplicate 二份（指副本）
   3 Copies ＝ 3 Folds ＝ Triplicate 三份（指副本）
   4 Copies ＝ 4 Folds ＝ Quadruplicate 四份（指副本）
   5 Copies ＝ 5 Folds ＝ Quintuplicate 五份（指副本）
2. Bear：（記載）此處用現在分詞 Bearing 修飾前面 Commercial invoice。
3. If any：意思是（如果有的話），此處是指如果有內盒。
   If possible 則是（如果可能的話）。

▌範例七

Signed invoices in triplicate showing separately the price and net weight in kgs. of each type of goods, name of carrying vessel as well as name and nationality/origin of manufacturers or producers of each item of manufactured or produced goods.

翻譯

有適當簽名的發票三份，分別地記載每一種商品的價格，及以公斤表示的淨重、船名，以及製造商或生產者的名稱，及國籍或原產地。

解說

1. Show：（顯示、表示）在此是記載的意思，Showing separately... 是分詞片語，修飾 Invoice，意為記載……的發票。

2. Triplicate：（一式三份的）
   例如：Drawn up in triplicate（做成一式三份的）

3. Manufacturer：（製造商）
   而 Producer 是（生產者），兩者不同在於，前者使用機器設備來製造商品的公司，而後者不一定會使用任何機器來生產，例如：農夫，他是 Producer 不是 Manufacturer。Manufacturer 生產的東西叫 Manufactured goods，而 Producer 生產的東西叫 Produced goods。

▌ 範例八

All the required certificates and declarations must be authenticated by the Chamber of Commerce and legalized by Saudi Arabian Consulate if available at beneficiary's country.

翻譯

所有需要的證明書及聲明書，都必須經過商會的認證，而且如果在受益人的國內，有沙烏地阿拉伯領事館的話，也須經其簽證。

解說

1. Authenticate：（證明……為真確、認證）
2. Legalize：（予以法律上的認可）亦即合法化。
3. If available：（如果可以利用的話）亦即如果有的話。

▌ 範例九

經常發生之信用狀修改條款列舉如下：

1. 裝運日期及信用狀有效期限之延長。

Shipment and validity extended to March 31, 2022 and April 15, 2022 respectively.

Shipment and validity both extended to March 31, 2022.

2. 更換出口商名稱及地址。

Beneficiary name and address changed to read _____ instead of previously stipulated.

3. 金額與貨物之增減。

L/C increased (decreased) by US$ _____ to US$ _____ and quantity of commodities increased (decreased) by _____ to _____ .

4. 保險種類之變換。

Insurance covering All Risks instead of ICC (B).

5. 裝運卸貨地點之更改。

Shipment from _____ to _____ instead of previously stipulated.

6. 提單抬頭人之修改。

B/Ls made out (to order of) _____ instead of previously stipulated.

7. 單據提示期限之修改。

Documents to be presented within 20 days after the date of issuance of shipping documents instead of previously stipulated.

8. 准予分批裝運。

Partial shipments permitted.

9. 准予轉運：只准限於某地轉運。

Transhipment permitted.

Transhipment at _____ permitted.

10. 刪掉檢驗報告（或某條款）。

Delete inspection report.

11. 貿易交貨條件由 CIF 改爲 FOB。

Trade terms amended to be on FOB basis instead of CIF.

12. 保險費及運費改由開狀申請人負擔。

Insurance premium and freight to be paid by applicant.

13. 裝載港不符。

Port of loading not complied with L/C stipulated.

14. 單據間重量互相矛盾。

Weights differ between documents.

Unit 13

歐盟國家在信用狀或訂單上對 G.S.P. Form A 的要求

■ 範 例

Certificate of People's Republic of China origin as per G.S.P. Form A, issued and manually signed by an authority, also manually signed by exporter bearing a reference number and showing exported to Austria. In case of shipment from Hong Kong evidencing the following in column 4: "This is to certify that the goods stated in this certificate had not been subjected to any processing during their stay/transhipment in Hong Kong" dated, stamped and signed by China Inspection Company Ltd.

翻譯

需要有中華人民共和國的 Form A，Form A 要由有關單位簽發及簽字，而且也要有出口廠商的簽字，Form A 上面要記載備案號碼及顯示出口到奧地利。

如果貨物要從香港裝船出口，Form A 的第四欄必須加註下列條文：「茲證明在本證明書上所記載的貨物，在香港停留及轉運期間未曾再加工處理，這個證明要由中國檢驗公司簽字、蓋章及加註日期。」

解說

1. G.S.P. Form A：英文全名為 Generalized system of preference certificate of origin Form A，簡稱 G.S.P. Form A 或僅稱 Form A。中文在臺灣稱為「優惠關稅產地證明書」，在中國大陸則叫做「普惠制產地證明書」。

2. Authority：（公共事業機構）
此處指 Form A 的簽發單位──「出入境檢驗檢疫局」。

3. Bear：（記載）
此處用現在分詞 Bearing 修飾前面的 Form A。

4. Reference No.：（備案號碼）
這個號碼是由申請 Form A 的廠商，在檢驗檢疫局核發的「產地註冊登記證」上面的註冊號，加上申請日期的流水號碼所組成。

5. Showing：（顯示）
用法與前面的 Bearing 一樣，都在修飾 Form A。

6. Column 4：（第四欄）
此處指 Form A 上面的第四欄位（請參閱附件）。

7. The goods stated in this certificate had not been subjected to any processing...：
這一句的主詞是 The goods，Stated 是過去分詞用以形容 The goods，動詞則是 Be subjected to（遭受），此處使用過去完成式的被動語態，表示這批貨物未受到加工之意。

8. Process：（加工）

   使用動名詞 Processing 作為 Be subjected to 的受詞。

9. During their stay/transhipment in Hong Kong ：

   Their 指的是這批貨物。

10. China Inspection Company Ltd.：（中國檢驗公司）

   此處指駐在香港的「中國檢驗公司」。

11. Dated, stamped and signed by China Inspection Company Ltd.：

   Dated、Stamped 及 Signed 都是使用被動式，表示（以上的條文）要被中國檢驗公司註明日期、蓋章及簽字。

附件

歐盟國家對 Form A 規定的 L/C 實例。

```
                                          091   DATE: JULY 10 2000

   Beneficiary
                                       Our advice No.

   AKING TRADING CO. LTD
   P.O.BOX 58425
   9F-2, 110 JEN AI ROAD, SEC 4
   TAIPEI, TAIWAN                       OSN: 887898         PAGE: 2


   ***  CONTINUED  ***
        AT USD 3,05/SET
     :
     CIF SALZBURG (AS PER INCOTERMS)
   46A(DOCUMENTS REQUIRED):
     1) COMMERCIAL INVOICE, 3-FOLD, ALL DULY SIGNED
     2) FULL SET CLEAN ON BOARD COMBINED TRANSPORT BILLS OF
        LADING
        MADE OUT TO ORDER, BLANK ENDORSED,
        MARKED 'FREIGHT PREPAID',
        NOTIFY:
        SPEDITION MULTICOM, A-5033 SALZBURG
          PHONE: 0662 641705, FAX: 451641
        AND APPLICANT
     3. PACKING LIST, 3-FOLD
        SHOWING MARKING AND CONTENTS OF THE CARTONS, CONTAINER
        AND ACCORDING CONTAINER NUMBER
     4. INSPECTION CERTIFICATE OF LOBECK CONCEPT AG
     5. GS/TUEV CERTIFICATE
        SHOWING MAX. 80 KG
     6. CERTIFICATE OF PEOPLE'S REPUBLIC OF CHINA ORIGIN
        AS PER GSP FORM A,
        ISSUED AND MANUALLY SIGNED BY AN AUTHORITY
        ALSO MANUALLY SIGNED BY EXPORTER BEARING A REFERENCE
        NUMBER AND SHOWING EXPORTED TO AUSTRIA
        IN CASE OF SHIPMENT FROM HONG KONG EVIDENCING THE
        FOLLOWING IN COLUMN 4:
        'THIS IS TO CERTIFY THAT THE GOODS STATED IN THIS
        CERTIFICATE HAD NOT BEEN SUBJECTED TO ANY PROCESSING
        DURING THEIR STAY/TRANSSHIPMENT IN HONG KONG'
        DATED, STAMPED AND SIGNED BY CHINA INSPECTION COMPANY
        LTD.
     7. INSURANCE CERTIFICATE OR POLICY FOR THE INVOICE VALUE
        PLUS 10 PERCENT, ENDORSED IN BLANK, COVERING
        ICC (A) WAR RISKS AS PER IWC (CARGO) INST. STRIKE CLAUSES
        CARGO, FROM SELLER'S WAREHOUSE TO BUYER'S WAREHOUSE
        CLAIMS PAYABLE IN AUSTRIA, NAMING A CLAIM SETTLING AGENT
        IN AUSTRIA.
     8. CERTIFICATE WITH ORIGINAL/COPY OF COURIER RECEIPT
        CERTIFYING THAT PHOTOCOPIES OF THE FOLLOWING DOCUMENTS
        HAVE BEEN SENT TO APPLICANT BY COURIER SERVICE: INVOICE,
        PACKING LIST, B/L, GSP FORM A AND INSURANCE CERTIFICATE
   47A(ADDITIONAL CONDITIONS):
     + UPON RECEIPT OF DOCUMENTS STRICTLY COMPLYING WITH CREDIT TERMS


              ***  TO BE CONTINUED NEXT PAGE  ***
```

Form A 第四欄實例。

GINAL　　　　　　　562493

1. Goods consigned from (Exporter's business name, address, country)	Reference No.　D432/00/0147
░░░░ PLASTICS (SHENZHEN) CO., LTD, SHENZHEN, CHINA	GENERALIZED SYSTEM OF PREFERENCES CERTIFICATE OF ORIGIN (Combined declaration and certificate) FORM A Issued in　THE PEOPLE'S REPUBLIC OF CHINA ------------------------------------ (country) See Notes overleaf
2. Goods consigned to (Consignee's name, address, country) ░░░░░░░░░░░░░░ 59700 MARCQ EN BAROEUL FRANCE	
3. Means of transport and route (as far as known) FROM SHEN ZHEN TO HONGKONG BY TRUCK ON/AFTER JUL. 04, 2000. THENCE TRANSHIPPED TO FRANCE VIA ANTWERP BY SEA	4. For official use THIS IS TO CERTIFY THAT THE GOODS STATED IN THIS CERTIFICATE HAD NOT BEEN SUBJECTED TO ANY PROCESSING DURING THEIR STAY/TRANSHIPMENT IN HONG KONG SIGNATURE:

5. Item number	6. Marks and numbers of packages	7. Number and kind of packages; description of goods	8. Origin criterion (see Notes overleaf)	9. Gross weight or other quantity	10. Number and date of invoices
	ACCENT ANTWERP C-NO. 19-173 1C-384 MADE IN CHINA	ZIPPERED BAGS (PVC) ACCORDING TO PROFORMA INVOICES NO CY15942 DATED 000531 AND CY15963R1 DATED 000608	"W" 19.23	41,156PCS	0147 JUL. 14, 2000
		SAY TOTAL FIVE HUNDRED AND FIFTY NINE (559) CTNS ONLY** L/C NUMBER 4460942011001H FRANCE AS COUNTRY OF DESTINATION			

| 11. Certification

It is hereby certified, on the basis of control carried out, that the declaration by the exporter is correct.

SHEN ZHEN
Place and date, signature and stamp of certifying authority | 12. Declaration by the exporter

The undersigned hereby declares that the above details and statements are correct; that all the goods were produced in ░░░░░ (country) and that they comply with the origin requirements specified for those goods in the Generalized System of Preferences for goods exported to FRANCE (importing country)

SHENZHEN JUL. 14, 2000
Place and date, signature of authorized signatory |

Unit
14　中國大陸常用的貿易合同範例

▌ 範　例

PURCHASE CONTRACT　　CONTRACT NO:
　　　　　　　　　　　　DATE:
The Seller:　　　　　　　The Buyer:
Add:　　　　　　　　　　Add:
Tel:　　　　　　　　　　Tel:
Fax:　　　　　　　　　　Fax:

Whereby the Seller agree to sell and the Buyer agree to buy
the under mentioned commodity(ies) according to the terms
and conditions stipulated below :

1. Name of Commodity, Specification & Packing	Quantity	Unit Price	Total Value
TOTAL: REMARKS:			

2. Shipping Mark(s):

On each package shall be stenciled conspicuously: Port of destination, package number, gross and net weights/ measurement, the shipping mark shown on the right side (for dangerous and/or poisonous cargo, the nature and generally adopted symbol shall be marked conspicuously on each package.)

3. Insurance: To be covered by the Seller for _____ % of the total invoice value against _____ risks.

Should the Buyer desire to cover for other risks besides the afore-mentioned or for an amount exceeding the afore-mentioned limit, the Seller's approval must be obtained first and all additional premium charges incurred therewith shall be for the Buyer's account.

4. Port of Shipment:

5. Port of Destination:

6. Time of Shipment:

7. Terms of Payment:

8. Shipping Documents: The seller shall present the following documents to the negotiating bank for payment:

(1) Full set of clean on board Bill of Lading made out to order and blank endorsed marked "Freight Prepaid".

(2) _____ copies of the invoice.

(3) _____ copies of the packing list(s) or weight memos.

(4) One original and _____ duplicate copies of the Transferable Insurance Policy or Insurance Certificate.

(5) One original and _____ duplicate copies of the Certificate of Quality, Quantify/Weight issued by _____ .

9. Inspection: The Certificate of Quantity/Weight issued by _____ shall be taken as the basis of delivery.

10. Force Majeure: The Seller shall not be held responsible for they owing to force majeure cause or causes, fail to make delivery within the time stipulated in the Contract or cannot deliver the goods. However, in such a case, the Seller shall inform the Buyer immediately by cable or Fax and if it is requested by the Buyer. The Seller shall also deliver to the Buyer by registered letter, a certificate attesting the existence of such a cause or causes.

11. Discrepancy and Claim: In case the Seller fail to ship the whole lot or part of the goods within the time stipulated in this Contract, the Buyer shall have the right to cancel the part of the Contract which has not been performed 30 days following the expiry of the stipulated time of shipment, unless there exists a Force Majeure

cause or the contract stipulation has been modified with the Buyer's consent.

In case discrepancy on the quality of the goods is found by the Buyer after arrival of the goods at the port of destination, the Buyer may, within 30 days after arrival of the goods at the port of destination, lodge with the Seller a claim which should be supported by an Inspection Certificate issued by a public surveyor approved by the Seller. The Seller, on the merits of the claim, either make good the loss sustained by the Buyer or reject their claim. It being agreed that the Seller shall not be held responsible for any loss or losses due to natural cause or causes falling within the responsibility of Ship-owners, or the Letter of Credit opened by Buyer does not correspond to the contract terms, and that the Buyer fail to amend thereafter its terms in time after receipt of notification by the Seller. The Seller shall have the right to cancel the contract or to delay the delivery of the goods and shall have also the right to claim for compensation or losses against the Buyer.

12. Arbitration: Any dispute arising from the execution of or in connection with this Contract should be settled through negotiation. In case no settlement can be

reached, the case shall then be submitted to the Foreign Trade Arbitration Commission of the China Council for the Promotion of International Trade, Peking for settlement in accordance with the Commissions Provisional Rules of Procedure. The award rendered by the Commission shall be final and binding on both parties.

13. Obligations: Both the Signers of this Contract, i.e. the Seller and the Buyer as referred to above, shall assume full responsibilities in fulfilling their obligations as per the terms and conditions herein stipulated. Any dispute arising from the execution of or in connection with this Contract shall be settled in accordance with terms stipulated above between the Signers of this Contract only, without involving the third party.

14. The Contract of a document makes _____ carbon copies. Each takes _____ copies of it.

Seller: _____ Buyer: _____

翻譯

購貨合同   合同編號：

日期：

賣方：   買方：

地址：   地址：

電話：   電話：

傳真：   傳真：

雙方同意按照本合同所列條款由賣方出售，買方購進下列貨物：

1. 商品名稱、規格及包裝	數量	單價	總價
總計： 備註：			

2. 裝運嘜頭：

   每件貨物上應註明到貨口岸、件號、每件毛重及淨重、尺碼及右列嘜頭（如係危險及／或有毒貨物，應按慣例在每件貨物上明顯列出有關標記及性質說明）。

3. 保險：由賣方按發票總值的＿＿＿％投保＿＿＿＿＿＿＿險，如買方欲增加其他險別或超過上述額度保險時，須事先徵得賣方同意，其增保費用由買方負擔。

4. 裝船口岸：

5. 目的地口岸：

6. 裝船期限：

7. 付款條件：

8. 裝運單據：賣方應向議付銀行（臺灣稱為押匯銀行）提供下列單據：

   (1) 全份裝船清潔提單抬頭空白背書，註明運費已付。

   (2) 發票＿＿＿份。

   (3) 裝箱單或重量單＿＿＿份。

   (4) 可轉讓的保險單或保險憑證正本一份及副本＿＿＿份。

   (5) ＿＿＿＿＿＿簽發的品質、數量、重量檢驗證正本一份，副本＿＿＿份。

9. 商品檢驗：由＿＿＿＿＿＿所簽發的數量、重量檢驗證，將作為交貨的依據。

10. 不可抗力：由於人力不可抗拒事故，使賣方不能在合同規定期限內交貨或者不能交貨，賣方不負擔責任，但賣方應立即以電報或傳真通知買方，如果買方提出要求，賣方應以掛號函向買方提供證明上述事故存在的事實。

11. 異議索賠：如果賣方不能在合同規定期限內把整批或一部分的貨物裝上船，除非人力不可抗拒原因，或取得買方同意而修改合同規定外，買方有權在合同裝船期滿30天後撤消未履行部分的合同。如果貨到目的地口岸買方對品質有異議時，可以憑賣方同意的公證機構出具的檢驗報告，在貨到目的地口岸30天內向賣方提出索賠，賣方將根據實際情況考慮理賠或不理賠。雙方同意一切損失凡由於自然原因或屬於船方責任範圍內者，賣方不必負責。如果信用狀在合同規定的日期內未送達賣方，或信用狀內容不符合同內容，並在買方收到賣方通知後無法及時修改信用狀條款，賣方將有權取消合同或延期交貨，並有權向買方索賠。

12. 仲裁：凡因執行本合同或有關本合同所發生的一切爭執，對方應協商解決，如果協商不能得到解決，應提交北京中國國際貿易促進會對外仲裁委員會，根據該仲裁委員會的仲裁程序暫行規則進行仲裁，仲裁決議是終局的，對雙方都有約束力。

13. 責任：簽約雙方，即上述賣方及買方，應對本合同條款全部負責履行，凡因執行本合同或有關本合同所發生的一切爭執，應由簽約雙方根據本合同規定解決，不涉及第三者。

14. 本合同正本一式＿＿＿份，雙方各執＿＿＿份。

賣方簽章：＿＿＿＿＿＿＿　　買方簽章：＿＿＿＿＿＿＿

解說

1. Contract：（契約、合同）
   中國大陸所謂的進出口貿易合同（Contract）有二個，一個叫做購貨合同（Purchase contract），另一個叫做銷貨合同（Sales contract），也就是我們所稱的購貨合約及銷貨合約。

2. Whereby：（藉此）用作副詞＝ By which
   傳統上合約的起頭有「買賣雙方基於善意藉此合約……」之意。

3. Stencil：（用鏤版刷印）
   以前木質包裝上面的字樣大都用鏤版刷印，不易脫落，在本文中可作爲「標明」（Mark）之意。

4. Conspicuously：（顯著地）

   例如：Judy makes herself conspicuous.

   （Judy 以奇裝異服引人注目。）

5. Generally：（普遍地）＝ Widely

6. Adopted：（被採用的）

7. Should the buyer desire to cover for other risks...：

   這裡的 Should ＝ If 是假設子句的開頭，主要句子的主詞是 The seller's approval 及 All additional premium charges incurred therewith...。

   這句中的 All additional 及 Incurred therewith 都在描述修飾 Premium charges。

8. For the buyer's account：＝ At the buyer's expense（由買方付帳）

9. Full set of clean on board Bills of Lading：

   （全套貨物已裝運上船的清潔提單。）

10. Transferable insurance policy or insurance certificate：

    Insurance policy 是保險單，簡稱保單，係證明保險人與被保險人之間成立保險契約的正式文件，載明雙方當事人所約定的權利、義務。

    而 Insurance certificate 是保險證明書，係保險人與被保險人之間訂有 Open policy（預約保險契約）時，當貨主（被保險人）向保險公司（保險人）通報每批貨物的裝運資料時，由保險公司所開立，證明貨物已由某一 Open policy 承保的證明書，由於 Insurance policy 與 Insurance certificate 具有相同的效力，因此 L/C 上大都規定 "Insurance policy or certificate"，只要受益人提出任何一種均可被接受。

11. Force majeure：（不可抗力），例如：地震、颱風等。

12. The seller shall not be held responsible for they owing to force majeure cause or causes, fail to make delivery within the time stipulated in the contract or cannot deliver the goods. ：

這個句子很長，因為包括一個主要句子 The sellers shall not be held responsible for，及兩個子句 They fail to make delivery... 及 They cannot deliver the goods。

另外再加上介系詞片語 Owing to force majeure cause or causes 來表示原因，Owing to（起因於）。

13. In such a case, the seller shall inform the buyer immediately by cable or fax and if it is requested by the buyer, shall also deliver to the buyer by registered letter, a certificate attesting the existence of such a cause or causes. ：

這句子很長，主要句子是 The sellers shall inform the buyers immediately by cable or fax. 及 The seller shall also deliver to the buyers by registered letter.

A Certificate...，後面的 Attesting the existence of such a cause or causes 是現在分詞用於修飾 A certificate。

14. Lodge with：（提出）＝ Present to

例如：I presented a complaint against her to the police.

（我針對她向警察提出抱怨控訴。）

15. Public surveyor：（公證人）或（公證機關）

16. On the merits of the claim：（依據索賠本身的是非曲直），

Merits 在法律上條文解釋為「真相」。

17. Make good the loss：（賠償損失）

　　Make good ＝ Compensate（賠償）

18. It being agreed：這是文法上的被動進行式，整句是 It is being agreed 省略 Is，「正在被同意著」之意。

19. Falling within：（屬於）

20. Correspond to：（符合）

21. Sustain ＝ Suffer：（承受、遭受）損害等。

22. In case no settlement can be reached, the case shall then be submitted to the foreign trade arbitration commission of the China Council for the Promotion of International Trade, Peking for settlement in accordance with the Commission's Provisional Rules of Procedure：

　　這句的主要句子是 The case shall then be submitted to...，而 In case no settlement can be reached 是假設子句。

　　The China Council for the Promotion of International Trade, Peking 是北京的「中國貿促會」類似臺灣的外貿協會。

23. The award rendered by the commission shall be final and binding on both parties：

　　Award（裁決書）是句中的主詞，動詞是 Shall be，而 Rendered by the commission 則是過去分詞用於修飾 Award。

　　Both parties 指買賣雙方。

24. Binding：（有拘束力的）

　　例如：The agreement is binding on all parties.

　　　　　（這協議對所有當事人具有拘束力。）

25. i.e. ＝ That is（即，換言之）

Unit 15　國貿條規（**Incoterms 2020**）交貨條件要點說明

第一項　**2020 國貿條規交貨條件中、英文名稱**

1. Terms for any mode or modes of transport（任何或多種運送方式的規則）

英文名稱	中文名稱
EXW Ex Works (Insert named place of delivery)	工廠交貨條件規則（加填指定交貨地）
FCA Free Carrier (Insert named place of delivery)	貨交運送人條件規則（加填指定交貨地）
CPT Carriage paid to (Insert named place of destination)	運費付訖條件規則（加填指定目的地）
CIP Carriage and insurance paid to (Insert named place of destination)	運保費付訖條件規則（加填指定目的地）
DPU Delivered at place unload (Insert named place of destination)	目的地卸載交貨規則（加填指定目的地）
DAP Delivered at place (Insert named place of destination)	目的地交貨條件規則（加填指定目的地）
DDP Delivered duty paid (Insert named place of destination)	稅訖交貨條件規則（加填指定目的地）

2. Rules for sea and inland water way transport（海運及內陸水路運送的規則）

英文名稱	中文名稱
FAS Free alongside ship (Insert named port of shipment)	船邊交貨條件（加填指定裝船港）
FOB Free on board (Insert named port of shipment)	船上交貨條件規則（加填指定裝船港）
CFR Cost and freight (Insert named port of shipment)	運費在內條件規則（加填指定裝船港）
CIF Cost, insurance and freight (Insert named port of shipment)	運保費在內條件規則（加填指定目的港）

第二項　交貨要點及主要運費分攤

Incoterms 2020（國貿條規 2020）

Cost distribution between seller & buyer（賣方及買方費用分攤）

S = Seller pays, B = Buyer pays（S ＝賣方付，B ＝買方付）

	EXW	FCA	FAS	FOB	CFR	CPT	DPU	DAP	DDP
1. Loading at seller's premises（在賣方營業場所裝貨）	B	S	S	S	S	S	S	S	S
2. Domestic precarriage/local cartage (after deliver to carrier)〔當地貨車運費（貨物交給運送業者之後）〕	B	B	S	S	S	S	S	S	S
3. Contract of carriage and dispatch（運送契約及發運）	B	B	B	B	S	S	S	S	S

	EXW	FCA	FAS	FOB	CFR	CPT	DPU	DAP	DDP
4. Trade documentation in country of exportation （出口國家的貿易文件）	B	S	S	S	S	S	S	S	S
5. Customs clearance in country of exportation （出口國家的報關）	B	S	S	S	S	S	S	S	S
6. Export charges （出口費用）	B	S	S	S	S	S	S	S	S
7. Terminal handling charge at port of loading （裝貨港的裝卸費用）	B	B	B	S	S	S	S	S	S
8. Loading at carrier's terminal （船隻在碼頭的裝貨費用）	B	B	B	S	S	S	S	S	S
9. Transportation equipments and accessories （運輸器具及附件）	B	B	B	S	S	S	S	S	S
10. Transport (cargo) insurance （貨物運輸保險）	—	—	—	—	—	—	—	—	—
11. International main carriage （國際運輸費用）	B	B	B	B	S	S	S	S	S
12. Unloading at terminal （碼頭卸貨）	B	B	B	B	B	S	S	S	S
13. Terminal handling charge at port of discharge （卸貨港的裝卸費用）	B	B	B	B	B	S	S	S	S
14. Trade documentation in country of transit/importation （進口國貿易文件費）	B	B	B	B	B	B	B	B	S
15. Customs clearance in country of importation （進口國報關費）	B	B	B	B	B	B	B	B	S
16. Import charge （進口費用）	B	B	B	B	B	B	B	B	S

第三項　賣方風險及主要運費圖示

Seller's risk and main carriage（賣方風險及主要運費）

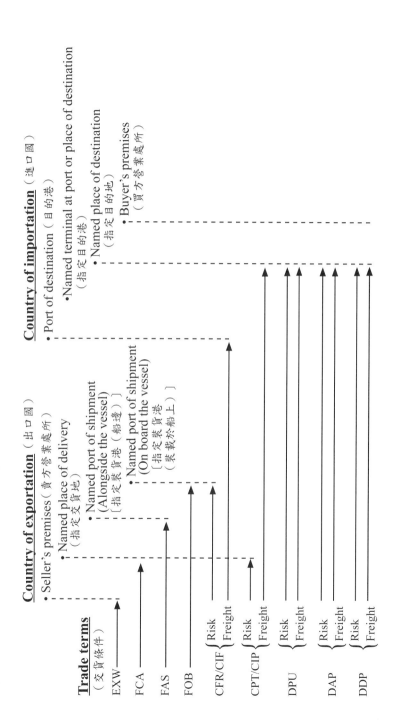

解說

1. Main difference between CFR and CPT:

   Under CFR rules, the risk of loss or damage to the goods passes when the goods are on board the vessel. Whereas, under CPT rules, the risk passes when the seller delivers the goods to the carrier or another person nominated by the seller.

   CFR 及 CPT 的主要差別
   - 風險：CFR 賣方將貨物裝載於船舶上，風險即移轉給買方，但 CPT 只要將貨物交付運送人時即行移轉。
   - 運費：CFR 出貨人付至指定目的港，CPT 付至指定目的地。

2. Main difference between CPT and DAP:

   Under CPT rules, the seller fulfills its obligation to deliver when it hands the goods over to the carrier.

   CPT 及 DAP 的主要差別
   - 風險：CPT 條件下，賣方將貨物在出口地交給指定運送人即行移轉，但 DAP 則要到指定目的地。
   - 運費：CPT 付到指定目的地，DAP 同樣付到指定目的地。

3. Main difference between DAP and DDP:

   Under DDP rules, the seller bears all risks and costs of import clearance.

   DAP 及 DDP 的主要差別在於 DDP 條件下，出貨人要承擔輸入報關手續及相關的費用（包括關稅、稅捐等）。

4. DPU 及 DAP 的主要差別：

DPU 規則下，賣方要承擔運費及風險，將貨物運送至目的地，並將貨物卸載交付給買方。

DAP 則是賣方僅需承擔運費及風險，將貨物運送至目的地交付買方即可。

5. Buyer's premises：（買方營業處所的交貨條件）

這是由買賣雙方自行約定的交貨方式，賣方要將貨物運送至買方的營業處所，也就是我們慣稱的 To door（到戶）的運送方式，國貿條規並無此交貨條件規則。

附錄

1 容易混淆的英文用詞釋義

1

Remitting bank：（託收銀行）
Collecting bank：（代收銀行）

在 D/A 及 D/P 的貿易付款條件下，出口商在貨物交運後，備妥運送單據，簽發以進口商為付款人的遠期匯票（D/P 則是即期匯票），一併委請本地託收銀行，寄往進口地指定的代收銀行，代向進口商提示匯票。如果是 D/A 條件，則進口商在匯票上承兌後，銀行即將運送單據交給進口商辦理提貨。如果是 D/P，則進口商必須付清票款後，代收銀行才會將運送單據交給進口商，我們稱本地的銀行為 Remitting bank，進口地的指定銀行為 Collecting bank。

2

Drawer：（出票人）
Drawee：（被出票人）

貨物運出口後，出口商根據 L/C 的規定，開立匯票向開狀銀行索取貨款，此時出口商為出票人（Drawer），開狀銀行或付款銀行為被出票人（Drawee），也就是匯票的付款人。而在 D/A、D/P 的付款條件下，匯票的 Drawee 則是進口商，不是代收銀行。

3

Advance of payment：（預付貨款）
Open account：（記帳）

當買賣雙方約定的付款方式是 Advance of payment 時，進口商必須先付清貨款，出口商才交運貨物，而在 Open account 的方式下，出口商必須先交運貨物，進口商才在付款期限到的時候，結付貨款。

4

Reimbursing bank：（補償銀行）
Claiming bank：（求償銀行）

補償銀行是指受開狀銀行委託，代其償付押匯銀行所代墊的押匯款項。而求償銀行則指銀行依信用狀規定，受理出口商的單據而為之付款，承兌或讓購後，有權向開狀銀行所指定的補償銀行，請求支付其所代墊的款項，該請求補償的銀行，稱為求償銀行，有可能是押匯銀行，或保兌銀行或付款銀行。〔付款銀行（Paying bank）可能是開狀銀行，也有可能是開狀銀行所委任或授權的另一銀行〕。

5

DDC ：Destination delivery charge（目的地移送費）
THC ：Terminal handling charge（貨櫃場處理費）

　　DDC 指北美航線到港貨櫃，從碼頭移送到貨櫃場內，或到內陸的火車場站所發生的費用，船公司向貨主收取，此費用項目稱爲目的地移送費。

　　而 THC 是指在貨櫃場內，貨櫃吊上、吊下及移動所產生的費用，同時也包含運送至港區裝船的拖車費用，由船公司向貨主收取，簡稱吊櫃費。

6

NVOCC ：Non-vessel operating common carrier（無船營運公共運送人）
Freight forwarder ：（貨運承攬商）

　　NVOCC 指提供海上運送服務，自訂運費表，以自己名義對貨主簽發提單，承擔運送責任的運送人，不論其是否擁有或經營該船舶。

　　NVOCC 對貨主而言是 Carrier（運送人），但對海洋運送人（實際擁有或經營船隻的運送人）而言，則是 Shipper（託運人）。

　　Freight forwarder 如果是以承攬運送人的身分，向貨主承攬貨物簽發提單收取運費，這種業者都泛稱爲 NVOCC。目前在臺灣的 Forwarder 都是此種性質。

7

MBS：Micro bridge service （微陸橋運輸）
MLB：Mini-land bridge service（迷你陸橋運輸）

　　MBS 是遠東運往美國內陸的貨櫃，在港口卸載後，由船公司代辦保稅運輸通關，負責將貨櫃經由鐵路或卡車，運往內陸各主要城市的貨櫃場，然後進口商在此辦理通關提貨手續，這種船公司提供的複合運送作業服務稱為 MBS，與 IPI 類似（Interior point intermodal，內陸點一貫運送）。

　　MLB 是遠東運往美國東岸的貨櫃，先在西岸的港口卸載，由船公司代辦保稅運輸通關，負責將貨櫃經由鐵路或卡車，運往東岸的港口或城市，進口商在此辦理通關提貨手續，這種結合海運貨櫃與陸路運輸的聯合作業，以節省海運繞道路程的運送方式稱為 MLB，中文亦稱為跨陸運送。

　　另經由水路繞道經過巴拿馬運河的運送方式，叫做全水路服務（All water service）。

8

All in：All inclusive （總價）
FAK ：Freight all kinds （品名無差別運費）

　　船公司或 Forwarder 的報價，若已包括海運運費及全部附加費用，叫 All in。

　　FAK 則是運費依貨物的體積或重量計算，不管其性質及種類。

■ 9

Shipped on board B/L：（裝運提單）
Received for shipment B/L：（備運提單）

　　裝運提單指貨物業已裝載於提單上標明之船舶的提單，Ocean
B/L 都屬於此種提單。

　　備運提單則指運送人收到貨物，尚未裝上運輸工具所簽發的
提單，此種提單上印有 "Received for shipment" 字樣，俟貨物實
際裝上運輸工具後，才蓋上 "On board" 的字樣，同時加上船名、
航次及 On board 日期。複合運送提單（Combined transport B/L），
如果信用狀不規定要 On board 時，船公司即簽發此類備運提單，
供貨主押匯使用。

■ 10-1

Normal rate：（正常運價）
Quantity rate：（高重量運價）

　　在空運的運費表中，貨物在 45 公斤級距以下者，適用的費
率叫 Normal rate，在提單中以 "N" 表示。45 公斤級距以上的貨
物所適用的費率叫 Quantity rate，在提單上以 "Q" 表示，這種運
價分 45 公斤、100 公斤、300 公斤、500 公斤等四種級距。

10-2

Revenue ton：（計費噸）
Measurement ton：（體積噸）

　　海運中船公司對於併櫃貨物的運費計算，當貨物的體積（以 CBM 表示）大於重量（以公斤表示）時，按體積重作為運費計算單位，此時 Measurement ton 就是 Revenue ton。如果貨物的重量噸（Weight ton）大於體積噸時，船公司則按重量噸作為 Revenue ton 來計算運費。

11

Volume weight：（材積重量）
Chargeable weight：（計價重量）

　　在空運中，航空公司對運費的計算，是比較 Gross weight（毛重）與 Volume weight（材積重量）何者為大，選擇較大者作為計價重量，此為 Chargeable weight。

　　Volume weight 的計算方式如下：

長 × 寬 × 高（CM）÷ 6,000 = V.W.

長 × 寬 × 高（IN）÷ 366 = V.W.

長 × 寬 × 高（M）= CBM（Cubic meter 材積噸）

1 CBM = 35,315 材

1 材 = 4.725 公斤

■ 12

UCP：Uniform Customs Practice for Documentary
Credit（信用狀統一慣例）
INCOTERMS：International Rules for the
Interpretation of Trade Terms（國貿條規）

　　兩者都是由國際商會所制定，UCP 是國際貿易信用狀交易的
規範，藉由該慣例的施行，信用狀各關係人之間的權利與義務，
始有較明確的界分。而 INCOTERMS 是針對國際貿易的交貨條
件，統一解釋規則，作為國際間貿易雙方簽訂買賣契約時的依
據。

■ 13

Break bulk cargo：（散裝貨物）
Bulky cargo：（龐大貨物）

　　散裝貨物是指直接裝載於船舶貨艙的貨物，沒有用貨櫃裝
載，與貨櫃貨物（Container cargo）是相對的名詞。
　　Bulky cargo 則是指體積大，佔大空間的貨物，與 Heavy cargo
（重貨）相對，不論是 Bulky cargo 或 Heavy cargo，都有可能是
Container cargo。如果直接裝運進貨艙的話，則又是 Break bulk
cargo。

14

Demurrage：（延滯費）
Detention charge：（留滯費）

就貨櫃運輸而言，進口的重櫃（內裝貨物），貨主沒有在 Free time（船公司給的免租費期間）內前往貨櫃場提領貨櫃，船公司對貨主加收的費用叫 Demurrage。而 Detention 則是貨主要出整櫃貨時，前往貨櫃場提領空櫃，以便在自己的工廠裝櫃，但未能在約定的時間（Free time）內歸還，船公司按日每櫃多少錢向貨主加收的費用。

簡言之，重櫃在貨櫃場，空櫃在貨主處超過 Free time，船公司加收的費用，前者叫 Demurrage，後者叫 Detention charge。

併櫃貨沒有此二費用，只有倉租費（Storage）。

15

Back to back L/C：（轉開信用狀）
Local L/C：（國內信用狀）

貿易商把國外 Buyer 開來以自己為受益人的信用狀（Original L/C 或稱 Master L/C），拿到自己有往來的外匯銀行作擔保，要求轉開以他人（通常是工廠）為受益人的信用狀，此信用狀稱為 Back to back L/C（轉開信用狀或背對背信用狀）。

若轉開給國外的供應商，則屬三角貿易型態，若轉開給國內的供應商，則屬國內貿易商向工廠採購的型態，此時這轉開的信用狀上面，買方、L/C 受益人及開狀銀行皆在國內，所以稱爲國內信用狀（Local L/C）。

Local L/C 與一般稱爲國內信用狀（Domestic L/C）不同的是，Local L/C 係由 Master L/C 轉開，而 Domestic L/C 是純粹由國內買主，向本地銀行要求開狀給國內供應商的中文信用狀。

▌ 16

Unrestricted L/C：（未限制押匯信用狀）
Restricted L/C：（限制押匯信用狀）

前者係指開狀銀行沒有在信用狀上特別指定押匯銀行的信用狀，受益人可以自行在有往來的銀行押匯，而後者 Restricted L/C，係指開狀銀行在信用狀上，有規定特定的銀行爲押匯銀行（常是 L/C 的通知銀行）。

L/C 上面如有下列條文，就可看出此信用狀爲 Restricted L/C：

"This credit is available with the advising bank by negotiation."，此時受益人需辦理轉押匯。

▌ 17

Sight L/C：（即期信用狀）
Usance L/C：（遠期信用狀）

前者係指開狀銀行於收到出口商經由押匯銀行寄來的匯票及押匯單據時即行付款，也就是所謂的見票即付，此種信用狀稱爲

Sight L/C。

而 Usance L/C 係指開狀銀行在信用狀上，有註明於收到出口商的匯票及押匯文件後，經過一段時日才付款，這種在匯票的到期日才付款的信用狀，稱為遠期信用狀，但進口商可先向開狀銀行取得裝船文件辦理報關提貨。

如果在這種信用狀上有載明 "Interest is for buyer's account" 或 "Discount charges are for account of buyer" 時，利息由買方負擔，此遠期信用狀稱為 Buyer's Usance L/C。反之，如 L/C 載明利息由賣方負擔，或 L/C 上根本沒有註明利息由何方負擔時，這遠期日數的利息即由賣方負擔，這種遠期信用狀稱為 Seller's usance L/C。

18

Full cable L/C：（詳電信用狀）
Brief cable L/C：（簡電信用狀）

電報信用狀（Cable L/C）能否直接押匯，可由電文來判斷："This is the operative credit instrument." 或 "No mail confirmation will follow."。

Cable L/C 有上列表示者，即為 Full cable 或 Full detail cable，出口商可以直接辦理押匯，否則即為 Brief cable 或 Preliminary cable，不可以直接押匯，必須等 Mail confirmation 到才能一起辦理押匯，此種 Cable 後面會註明 "Full details to follow" 或 "Airmailing details"。

▌19

OBU：（境外金融業務分行）
DBU：（外匯指定銀行）

　　OBU 英文全名爲 Off-shore Banking Unit，是國內銀行專爲經營境外金融業務而特別成立的分行（部門），每家銀行只能設立一個 OBU，例如：第一商銀在臺北設一個 OBU，其他都市就不能再設立 OBU 了。

　　由國外開來的 L/C 受益人如果是我們的境外公司，則此信用狀必須在 OBU 押匯。（請參考附件 L/C 實例）

　　DBU 就是一般經中央銀行指定辦理外匯業務的銀行，例如：三商銀、土銀、上海商銀……。

　　依規定外匯指定銀行只經營境內的外匯業務，所以稱爲 Domestic Banking Unit，簡稱 DBU，以便與經營境外業務的 OBU 區別。

▌20

Bank guarantee：（銀行保證函）
Stand-by L/C：（擔保信用狀）

　　銀行保證函是銀行應客戶的要求而開的保證函，如果被保證人（客戶）不履行付款或不履行契約義務時，由保證人（銀行）出面代爲付款或代爲履行契約。

　　擔保信用狀又稱爲保證信用狀，是銀行爲了保證客戶履行其債務內容，而以債權人為受益人所開發的，這種信用狀不以清償因商品交易而生的價款為目的，而是以融通資金或保證債務為目的所開發的信用狀。因此擔保信用狀所要求的單據，是由受益人所出具的聲明書或證明書，即可要求銀行付款，不必像一般 L/C 要求提供裝運單據。

　　由於銀行保證函的法律關係很複雜，一般都以擔保信用狀來辦理。

21

Back to back L/C：（轉開信用狀）
Transferable L/C：（可轉讓信用狀）

　　Back to back L/C 係中間貿易商憑國外開來的信用狀（Master L/C），向本地銀行申請另開一張信用狀以國內或國外之供應商為受益人的信用狀。這一轉開信用狀的金額通常較原信用狀小，有效期限也較原信用狀短，但數量及品質必須一致，以便調換相關的押匯單據。

　　而 Transferable L/C 係信用狀受益人，向轉讓銀行請求將信用狀之全部或一部分轉讓給另一個第二受益人。

　　Back to back L/C 之申請人，必須在轉開銀行持有授信額度，但 Transferable L/C 之申請人，在轉讓銀行不一定要有授信額度，轉讓銀行僅負責辦理轉讓手續或事後之換單手續而已，付款則由 Transferable L/C 開狀銀行負最後付款責任，所以轉讓銀行對 L/C 轉讓申請人是否有授信額度，並非必要條件。

22

Insurance policy：（保險單）
Insurance certificate：（保險證明書）
Open policy：（預約保單）

　　Insurance policy：（保險單）簡稱保單，係證明保險人與被保險人之間，成立保險契約的正式文件，載明雙方當事人所約定的權利、義務。

　　而 Insurance certificate 是（保險證明書），係在保險人與被保險人之間，訂有 Open policy（預約保單），當貨主（被保險人）向保險公司（保險人）通報每批貨物的裝運資料時，由保險公司所開立，證明貨物已由某一 Open policy 承保的證明書。

　　由於 Insurance policy 與 Insurance certificate 具有相同的效力，因此 L/C 上大都規定 "Insurance policy or certificate"，只要受益人提出任何一種，均可被接受。

補充說明

Open policy：（預約保單）
這是由保險公司（保險人）承保貨主（被保險人）在某一定期間如一年或半年　，所有須由被保險人負擔運輸保險的貨物，全部交由該預約保險人承保，而由保險公司所簽發的一項總括性保險契約，貨主只要在每一批貨物裝運確定時，將保險金額、貨物名稱、數量、船名、起運日期及起訖地點，向保險公司聲明，即完成手續。

23

Bill of lading（B/L）：（提單）
Delivery order（D/O）：（提貨單）

B/L 是運送人在出貨人（Shipper）的貨物裝船後，發給出貨人的收貨證明及運送契約。由於 B/L 具有物權證券的性質，可以經由背書而轉讓 B/L 上所記載的貨物，方便國際貿易買賣。

D/O 則是運送人在收貨人（Consignee）交還正本提單時，發給收貨人藉以報關提貨的憑證，為與 B/L 區別，提貨單亦被稱為小提單。D/O 不能背書轉讓，只有收貨人才能報關提貨，收貨人在報關提貨時，海關只看 D/O 不看 B/L。

24

Ocean bill of lading：（海洋提單）
Combined transport bill of lading：（複合運送提單）

1. 海洋提單的內容性質主要有以下二點：
   (1) 當信用狀要求港至港運送的提單時（例如：L/C 規定 Shipment from Keelung to Hamburg），提單上一定要表明信用狀規定的裝貨港及卸貨港，但提單上記載的收貨地如與裝貨港不同時，應於提單上加註：「裝貨港、裝載貨物的船名及裝載日期」。
   (2) 提單上要表明貨物業已裝載／裝運於標名之船舶，因為既然是港至港的運送，貨物一定是用船舶來裝載，所以要有船名及裝載日期（On board date）。

2. 複合運送提單的內容性質如下：

(1) 當信用狀要求涵蓋至少二種不同運送方式的單據時（例如：L/C 規定 Shipment from Hsin-chu to Frankfurt）。

所謂運送方式是指陸運、空運、水運或海運，只要這批貨在整個運送過程中使用到二種以上不同的運送方式，例如：陸、空或海、空或陸、海、空這就算複合運送。因為複合運送並不一定會用到海運，例如：使用陸、空方式，所以複合運送的提單並不一定要有船名或 On board date。

(2) 要表明貨物業已接管（Taken in charge）/ 發送（Despatched）/ 裝載（Shipped on board）的任何一項。

這裡的「接管」意思是貨主把貨交由運送人接管，「發送」則是指空運把貨裝上飛機的意思，如同海運的 Shipped on board。

當 L/C 要求複合運送提單要表示 Shipped on board 時，船公司一定要等到貨主的貨物實際已裝上船，才會簽發蓋有 "Loaded on board" 的提單給貨主，貨主押匯時也才不會有瑕疵。

(3) 表明信用狀規定的接管地及目的地，該接管地得不同於裝載港、機場或裝載地；該目的地得不同於卸貨港、機場或卸貨地。

例如：新竹的廠商接到 L/C 規定 "Shipment from Hsin-chu to Frankfurt"，很明顯的這將是複合運送，因為從新竹到德國法蘭克福不可能在整個運送過程中，只用到一種運送方式就可到達，一定要使用到二種以上不同的運送方式，因為新竹並不是機場或是裝貨港，只是出貨的裝載地而已。

Combined Transport B/L 亦稱為 Multi-modal Transport B/L。

🎯 附件

國外開來臺灣，受益人是境外公司的 L/C。

```
------------------- Instance Type and Transmission -----
Original received from SWIFT
Priority                : Normal
Message Output Reference : 0749 030416CCBCTWTPAXXX7173690047.
Correspondent Input Reference : 1832 030415MSBCCNBJA0042747135302
----------------------- Message Header -----------------
Swift Output   : FIN 700 Issue of a Documentary Credit
Sender         : MSBCCNBJ004
                 CHINA MINSHENG BANKING CORPORATION
                 (SHENZHEN BRANCH)
                 SHENZHEN CN
Receiver       : CCBCTWTPXXX
                 CHANG HWA COMMERCIAL BANK LTD.
                 TAIPEI TW
MUR : 2003041500139868
----------------------- Message Text -------------------
 27: Sequence of Total
     1/1
 40A: Form of Documentary Credit
     IRREVOCABLE
 20: Documentary Credit Number
     1813LC03000052
 31C: Date of Issue
     030415
 31D: Date and Place of Expiry
     030525IN TAIWAN
 50: Applicant
     ▬▬▬▬▬▬▬▬▬▬▬▬▬▬▬▬▬
     IMP.AND EXP. CO. LTD.
     SHENZHEN,CHINA
 59: Beneficiary - Name & Address
     ▬▬▬▬▬▬▬▬▬▬▬▬▬
     TOWN,TORTOLA BRITISH VIRGIN
     ISLANDS,C/O ▬▬▬▬▬▬▬ FU HSING
     N. RD.,TAIPEI,TAIWAN
 32B: Currency Code, Amount
     Currency       : USD (US DOLLAR)
     Amount         :         #205,000.00#
 41D: Available With...By... - Name&Addr
     ANY BANK
     BY NEGOTIATION
 42C: Drafts at...
     SIGHT FOR 100 PCT OF
     INVOICE VALUE SHOWING THIS L/C NO.
     AND DATE OF ISSUE
 42A: Drawee - BIC
     MSBCCNBJ004
     CHINA MINSHENG BANKING CORPORATION
     (SHENZHEN BRANCH)
     SHENZHEN  CN
 43P: Partial Shipments
     ALLOWED
 43T: Transhipment
     ALLOWED
```

（受益人是BVI的境外公司，L/c
由台北接受轉交）

```
16/04/03-07:48:17          OUTEXPD-1221-000002

√ 44A: On Board/Disp/Taking Charge at/f
       TAIWAN
√ 44B: For Transportation to...
       HONG KONG,DESTINATION HUIYANG
  44C: Latest Date of Shipment
       030515
  45A: Descriptn of·Goods &/or Services
       AIR CONDITIONING RELATED PRODUCTS AS PER ORDER NO.:TCC-3341
       TOTAL VALUE:USD205,000.00
  46A: Documents Required
       +SIGNED COMMERCIAL INVOICE IN 3 ORIGINALS INDICATING THIS L/C
        NO.,CONTRACT NO. AND ORDER NO.·
       +2/3 SET OF CLEAN ON BOARD OCEAN BILLS OF LADING MADE
        OUT TO ORDER AND BLANK ENDORSED, MARKED 'FREIGHT COLLECT' AND
        NOTIFY THE APPLICANT.
       +PACKING LIST IN 2 FOLDS ISSUED BY BENEFICIARY.
       +BENEFICIARY'S CERTIFIED COPY OF FAX SENT TO THE APPLICANT
        WITHIN 24 HOURS AFTER SHIPMENT ADVISING NAME OF VESSEL, DATE,
        QUANTITY, WEIGHT AND VALUE OF SHIPMENT.
       +BENEFICIARY'S CERTIFICATE CERTIFYING THAT 1/3 SET OF CLEAN ON
        BOARD BILLS OF LADING,2 ORIGINAL COMMERCIAL INVOICES AND 2
        ORIGINAL PACKING LISTS HAVE BEEN DISPATCHED TO THE APPLICANT
        BY·DHL.·
  47A: Additional Conditions
       +APPLICANT'S ADDRESS:▇▇▇▇▇▇▇▇▇▇▇▇▇▇▇▇▇▇▇▇▇▇▇▇
        ▇▇▇▇▇▇▇▇▇▇▇▇▇▇▇▇▇▇▇▇▇▇▇.,SHENZHEN,
        518031,P.R.CHINA.TEL:0086-755-▇▇▇▇▇▇▇
        FAX:0086-755-▇▇▇▇▇▇▇.
       +THE AMOUNT OF EACH DRAFT MUST BE ENDORSED ON THE REVERSE OF
        THIS CREDIT BY THE NEGOTIATING BANK.
       +A DISCREPANCY FEE OF USD50.00 OR EQUIVALENT IS FOR
        BENEFICIARY'S ACCOUNT WHICH WILL BE DEDUCTED FROM THE PROCEEDS
        ON EACH PRESENTATION OF DISCREPANT DOCUMENTS UNDER THIS
        CREDIT,IF ANY.
       +MULTI MODAL TRANSPORT B/L ACCEPTABLE.
  71B: Charges
       ALL BANKING CHARGES OUTSIDE
       ISSUING BANK ARE FOR APPLICANT'S
       ACCOUNT.
   48: Period for Presentation
       DOCUMENTS MUST BE PRESENTED WITHIN
       10 DAYS AFTER SHIPMENT DATE BUT
       WITHIN VALIDITY OF THIS CREDIT
   49: Confirmation Instructions
       WITHOUT
   78: Instr·to Payg/Accptg/Negotg Bank
       +UPON RECEIPT OF THE DOCUMENTS AND THE DRAFTS IN COMPLIANCE
        WITH THE TERMS AND CONDITIONS OF THIS CREDIT,THE REIMBURSEMENT
        WILL BE EFFECTED AS PER THE NEGOTIATING BANK'S INSTRUCTION.
       +ALL DOCUMENTS MUST BE SENT TO CHINA MINSHENG BANKING CORP.
        SHENZHEN BR.29/F.,B JIAHE HUAQIANG MANSION,HENNAN RD.,
        CENTRAL SHENZHEN 518031 P.R.CHINA IN ONE LOT BY DHL OR
        COURIER.
```

附錄

2　常用的船務英文專有名詞

1. **AI：All Inclusive（總價）**

   船公司的報價已包括基本運費及附加費等。

2. **ANERA：Asia North America Eastbound Rate Agreement（遠東北美東向運費協定）**

   航行遠東北美之間的船公司，為求運費穩定彼此間對運費的協議。

3. **BAF：Bunker Adjustment Factor（燃料附加費）**

   燃料價格調漲時，船公司營運成本會增加，為彌補此增加的成本，船公司會按變動的幅度，訂定一百分比隨著基本運費向貨主收取，有些船公司使用 FAF（Fuel Adjustment Factor）。

4. **Break-Bulk Cargo（散裝貨）**

   不是裝於貨櫃中的貨物，通常為大宗物品如水泥、穀物等。

5. **CAF：Currency Adjustment Factor（幣值調整附加費）**

   又稱美金貶值附加費，因船公司的運費大都以美金作為計價單位，當美金貶值時，船公司的運費收入就減少，為彌補此損失，船公司會按貶值的幅度，訂定一百分比，隨著基本運費向貨主收取。

6. CFS：Container Freight Station（貨櫃貨物集散站）

在貨櫃場內，貨物在此併櫃或拆櫃，由於併櫃貨（LCL）是貨主用卡車送來此處裝櫃，所以把併櫃貨也叫做 CFS。

7. CLP：Container Loading Plan（貨櫃裝貨明細表）

又稱 CLL（Container Loading List），記載貨櫃中所裝貨物的品名、箱數、目的港等。

8. CW：Chargeable Weight（計價重量）

空運運費的計算單位，是以毛重（Gross Weight）及體積重（Volume Weight）較大者作為計價的重量。

9. CY：Container Yard（貨櫃存放場）

在貨櫃場內有重櫃 CY 區及空櫃 CY 區，貨主要出整櫃貨（FCL）時，會派拖車到空櫃 CY 區領櫃子回工廠裝貨，再把此重櫃拖回貨櫃場的重櫃 CY 區等待裝船，所以一般也把整櫃貨叫做 CY。

10. DDC：Destination Delivery Charge（目的地移送費）

從卸貨港把貨櫃移送至貨櫃場或火車站所收的費用，一般由 Consignee（收貨人）支付。

11. Demurrage（貨櫃延滯費）

進口的重櫃放在貨櫃場的 CY 區，可能由於貨主（Consignee）尚未贖單報關等因素，以致此貨櫃超過船公司所給予的免租費期（Free Time），通常為 7 天，每超過一天船公司向貨主收取 NT\$400/20'、NT\$800/40'（各家船公司略有不同）作為貨主延滯此貨櫃的罰金。

12. Detention（貨櫃留滯費）

貨主（Shipper）向船公司拖空櫃回工廠裝貨，可能由於貨款尚未收到或者貨物有問題，以致此貨櫃一直滯留在貨主處，超過船公司給予的免租費期，船公司向貨主收取每超過一天 NT\$400/20'、NT\$800/40' 作為罰金（各家船公司略有不同）。

13. D/O：Delivery Order（提貨單）

運送人在收貨人交還正本提單時，發給收貨人藉以報關提貨的憑證，為與 B/L 區別，提貨單被稱為小提單。

14. EIR：Equipment Interchange Receipt（貨櫃交接驗收單）

貨櫃進出貨櫃場，檢驗櫃況的憑據，用來釐清貨櫃場與船方或貨主的責任。

15. ETA：Estimated Time of Arrival（預計船抵達的時間）

16. ETD：Estimated Time of Departure（預計船開航的時間）

由於天候、風浪等因素均足以影響船、飛機速度，因此無法預先公布準確的抵達或開航的日期時間，以免引發糾紛。

17. FAK：Freight All Kinds（不論品名的運費）

不論何種商品，其每一 CBM 或 1,000 公斤的運費都一樣（危險品除外）。

18. FCL：Full Container Load（整櫃貨）

裝滿一個貨櫃的貨。

19. Feeder Vessel（子船或稱支線集貨船）

跑近海的船隻，載運量較小，被用來作為母船運送貨櫃的交通船，這樣會比母船彎靠每一港口裝卸貨來得經濟、方便。

20. FI/FO：Free In / Free Out（船方不負責裝卸）

大宗貨物貨主與船公司接洽租船事宜承運貨物時，雙方在傭船契約上，訂明船方不負擔裝船費用即為 FI，不負擔卸船費用即為 FO。如果上述傭船契約訂明裝卸費用歸船方負擔，此條件即為 Berth Term，又稱為 Liner Term，好像定期船的貨物運送一樣，貨主不必負擔裝卸的費用。

21. GRI：General Rate Increase（基本運費調漲）

船公司全面調漲基本運費，通常以某百分比作為調高的幅度。

22. Groupage：（散貨併裝成整櫃）

把 LCL 併櫃貨併裝成 FCL 整櫃貨，也叫做 Consolidation。

23. HQ：High Cubic Container（高櫃）

指 9 呎半高的 40' 貨櫃。

24. HS：Harmonized Commodity Description and Coding System（調和商品分類制度）

我國稅則分類在民國 60 年採用「關稅合作理事會稅則分類」（Customs Cooperation Council Code，即 CCC CODE）。民國 78 年採用 HS，又稱為「國際商品統一分類制度」。

25. ICC：International Chamber of Commerce（國際商會組織）

總部設於法國巴黎的國際性機構，目的在公平地促進國際貿易的順利進行，大家所熟知的信用狀統一慣例及國貿條規係由 ICC 所制定。

26. IMDG Code：International Maritime Dangerous Goods Code

國際海事組織對海上運送危險品的規定。

27. IPI：Interior Point Intermodal（內陸點運送）

從臺灣運往美國的內陸城市的貨櫃，在美國西岸港口卸下後，由船公司負責安排卡車或火車運往內陸的目的地，收貨人在此辦理報關提貨；例如：船公司報價 IPI Chicago US$70/CBM，船公司會負責把貨送到 Chicago 貨櫃場，在此把貨交給收貨人。

28. LCL：Less-Than Container Load（併櫃貨）

不滿一個整櫃的貨。

29. L/I：Letter of Indemnity（切結書）

亦稱 Letter of Guarantee 保證書。

30. Manifest：（艙單）

船（飛機）上所載貨物的明細表或乘客的名單。

31. MLB：Mini Land Bridge（迷你陸橋跨陸運送）

由臺灣運往美國東岸的貨櫃，在美國西岸港口卸下後，由船公司負責安排火車或拖車橫越大陸，運到東岸的港口或城市，讓受貨人在此辦理報關提貨，這種運送方式稱為 MLB。有別於另一種叫做 All Water Service，即運往東岸的貨櫃，從遠東開始全程用船運，經過巴拿馬運河運抵東岸，這種方式耗時較久，約比 MLB 慢十天，但運費較便宜，大概 1×20' 相差 US$150。

32. PNW：Pacific Northwest

臺灣到北美太平洋西北岸航線，彎靠港有 Portland、Seattle、Vancouver。

33. PSW：Pacific Southwest

臺灣到北美太平洋西南岸航線，彎靠港有 Long Beach、Oakland。

34. TEU：Twenty-foot Equipment Unit（20 呎櫃等量單位）

又稱爲 20 呎標準貨櫃。1×20' 櫃稱爲一個 TEU，1×40' 櫃 ＝ 2 TEU。

35. THC：Terminal Handling Charge（貨櫃場處理費）

又稱爲吊櫃費，由貨主支付船公司，金額視各區域不同，例如：東南亞線 1×20' 櫃要 N\$5,600、1×40' 櫃則要 NT\$7,000。

常用的空運英文專有名詞及術語解釋

1. IATA：International Air Transportation Association 國際航空運輸
   協會。

2. Direct：直走。

3. Consol：Consolidation 併裝。

4. Transit：轉運。

5. MAWB：Master Airway Bill（主提單），亦指航空公司之提單。

6. HAWB：House Airway Bill（分提單），指空運公司之提單。

7. CNEE：Consignee（收貨人）。

8. SHPR：Shipper（寄貨人）。

9. Agent：國外代理。

10. PP：Prepaid 運費預付（指運費由寄貨人負擔）。

11. CC：Collect 運費到付（指運費由收貨人負擔）。

12. G.W.：Gross Weight（毛重）。

13. V.W.：Volume Weight（材積重）。

14. C.W.：Chargeable Weight（計價重量）。

15. Local Debit Note：通常指 PP 帳單。

16. Debit Note：通常指「應收」國外帳單。

17. Credit Note：通常指「應付」國外帳單。

18. Profit Share：專為利潤分配之帳單，包括「應收」和「應付」
    兩種。

19. IATA Rate：指國際航空運輸協會所規定之價格。

20. Selling Rate：指賣價。

21. Net Rate：指底價。

22. Net/Net Rate：指真正的底價。

23. All-in：指將所有費用全部計算在一起之報價。

〔即指預先將（運費＋其他費用＋報關費）÷ 重量後之單價作為報價之方式〕，採用這方式只能向付款者收取此 All-in 之價格，不可再收取其他費用，除非是客戶所要求代為申請之某項特殊文件費。

24. M：Minimum Charge（指最低收費）。

25. N：Normal Rate（－ 45KG，指 45KG 以下之費率）。

26. Q：Quantity Rate（＋ 45KG，指 45KG 以上之費率）。

27. Air freight：空運運費。

28. Freighter：全貨機。

29. W.S.C. (T/C)：Warehouse Charge (Terminal Charge) 倉租。

MIN. TWD100。300 公斤以下，每公斤 TWD5.00；超過 300 公斤，超過之部分每公斤 TWD1.50。

〔例如：重量為 520KGS，應付倉租 TWD1,830。即 TWD5.00 × 300KGS ＋ TWD1.50×（520KGS － 300KGS）〕。

30. EDIC：Electronic Data Interchange Charge 鍵輸費。

一般航空公司每張提單收費 TWD40.00，出口海關以時間計費，進口海關收費 TWD200.00（可依各公司之決定自行設定收費及成本標準）。

31. H/C：Handling Charge 手續費或報關費。

（可依各公司之決定自行設定收費及成本標準）。

32. Cartage：卡車費。

33. TACT：The Air Cargo Tariff 國際航空貨運規章。

34. ULD：Unit Load Devices 單位裝載器具，亦即空運盤櫃。

35. R/A：Restricted Articles 管制品。

36. D/G：Dangerous Goods 危險品。

37. Customs Airport：清關機場（有海關駐紮負責貨物通關的機場）。

38. Manifest：艙單（貨物申報單）。

有航空公司的艙單及空運公司的艙單。

39. C.A.S.：Customs Automation System 海關自動化通關系統。

40. Off Load：貨物從飛機上被拉下來。

（通常指途中 Space 擁擠時。）

41. C.O.D.：Cash On Delivery 貨到收款。

進口提單上如有註明 C.O.D. 意謂代收貨價的意思，此種送貨及兼收貨款的方式，大都用於進口商向國外買進急需的小量樣品，供應商請空運公司在進口地送貨時順便收款的方式，這樣可以節省時間，而空運公司也可從中賺取手續費。

42. C.A.D.：Cash Against Document 付款交單。

這是國際貿易中慣用的付款方式之一，空運進口提單如有註明 "Cash Against Document"，就是出口地的空運公司要提醒進口地的代理，在放貨時要注意提單上的 Consignee（通常是銀行）是否有簽名背書，有的話才可以放貨。

• 直飛：指該航線飛機直接由起運地飛抵目的地，中途不停靠其他機場。

例如：TPE － LAX　by　"CI"

• 轉機：指該航線飛機由起運地飛抵目的地，途中須至某一指定機場轉換另一班機。

例如：TPE － HKG　by　"CX435/02 MAR"

HKG － SHA　by　"KA808/03 MAR"

• 直走：指直接以航空公司之提單（Master Air Waybill）出貨，直走有可能直飛，也可能途中停靠某機場上下貨，但原機飛往目的地機場。

　　直走原因之一：

(1) 寄貨人或收貨人指定必須採用直走方式。

(2) L/C 指定必須採用航空公司之提單押匯。

(3) 空運公司在目的地沒有國外代理商代為處理，或無法併裝。

• 併裝：指將不同出貨人所出至「同一目的地」或「可先送至該目的地再行轉運」之貨，合併在一起當成一筆貨，或為「國外代理之指定貨」必須以併裝之方式出貨者，以一張主提單（MAWB）出貨之方式。空運公司發分提單（HAWB）給各出貨人。

　　併裝原因之一：

(1) 同時收到不同寄貨人出至同一目的地之貨，且無指定直走可藉由併裝獲取更多利潤。

(2) 運費為到付（Collect）且收費低於 IATA Rate，須由 Agent 代收運費。

(3) 航空公司拒收 Collect 貨。

(4) 指定貨（Routing Order）指定必須由某一空運公司或國外代理商代為運送。

(5) 三角貿易商（避免製造廠商和收貨人直接接觸）。

(6) 轉運貨（須由國外代理商安排轉運至目的地）。

附錄

3 容易混淆的英文句型及其用法

第一項 及物動詞與不及物動詞

一 及物動詞：又分為完全及物動詞及不完全及物動詞。

1. 完全及物動詞：因為及物，所以後面一定要有受詞，句子的意思才完整，其基本句型為：

主詞＋動詞＋受詞

而作為完全及物動詞的受詞有：

(1) 名詞或代名詞。例如：I love <u>Judy</u>.（名詞）、I need <u>you</u>.（代名詞）

(2) 動名詞。例如：I enjoy <u>dancing</u>.（動名詞）

(3) 不定詞。例如：He wants <u>to see me</u>.（不定詞）

(4) 名詞子句。例如：I know <u>that he is a rich man</u>.（名詞子句）

(5) 名詞片語。例如：I do not know <u>how to do it</u>.（名詞片語）

補充說明

所謂名詞子句是以 That、Whether 及疑問詞（如 When、What、How 等）開頭所引導的句子，而名詞片語係由「疑問詞＋不定詞片語」所形成，只有片語，不像子句有主詞、動詞等完整的句子。例如：What to buy、

> Whom to see。由於名詞子句及名詞片語，均具有名詞的
> 功能，故可作爲及物動詞的受詞。

2. 不完全及物動詞：因屬及物動詞，後面也是要有受詞，但加
上受詞之後，句子的意思還是不夠完整，所以需要補語，語
意才會完全，又因爲此補語係在修飾受詞，所以叫做受詞補
語，其基本句型爲：

　　　主詞＋動詞＋受詞＋受詞補語

可作爲受詞補語的有：
(1) 形容詞。例如：He makes me <u>happy</u>.（他使我快樂。）
(2) 名詞。例如：He is <u>a good student</u>.
(3) 不定詞。例如：He asked me <u>to come</u>.
(4) 現在分詞（表主動進行狀態時）。例如：I saw him <u>parking</u>
<u>his car</u> when I arrived.
(5) 過去分詞（表被動的概念時）。例如：I saw the car <u>parked</u>
when I arrived.
(6) 地方副詞（諸如 In、Out、Home、Here、There 等，作爲
Be 動詞之後的補語）。例如：He is <u>here</u>.

■ 不及物動詞：又分完全不及物動詞及不完全不及物動詞。

1. 完全不及物動詞：此類動詞的後面不必加上受詞，句子的意
思就已完全，其基本句型爲：

　　　主詞＋動詞

例如：The sun rises.（太陽出來。）即「日出」之意。

He studied abroad last year.（他去年在國外念書。）

2. 不完全不及物動詞：屬於不及物動詞，當然後面不必加受詞，但只有主詞及動詞，句子的語意不完整，所以需要補語來讓意思完整，又因為此補語係在修飾主詞，所以又稱為主詞補語，其基本句型為：

主詞＋動詞＋主詞補語

可做主詞補語的有：

(1) 名詞或代名詞。例如：He becomes a <u>rich man</u>.

(2) 形容詞。例如：I feel <u>comfortable</u>.

(3) 動名詞。例如：Seeing is <u>believing</u>.

(4) 不定詞。例如：He seems <u>to read the letter</u>.

(5) 名詞子句。例如：It appears <u>that we have not received your L/C</u>.

(6) 名詞片語。例如：I don't know <u>what to buy</u>.

---○ 補充說明 ○---

不完全不及物動詞──主要及常見的此類動詞有：

a. Be 動詞（Is、Am、Are）。例如：He is handsome.

b. 感官動詞（Look、Smell、Taste、Sound、Feel）。例如：She looks pretty.

c. 連綴動詞（Appear、Seem、Remain、Become）。

d. Get、Turn（變成）。例如：He gets angry. / Her face turns red.

如何分辨及物動詞與不及物動詞

（註：此部分係參考常春藤出版《英文文法》）

把動詞套進此公式：我＿＿＿＿你、你被我＿＿＿＿

套進去後，如果句子的語意清楚，此動詞應是及物動詞，如果語意矛盾或沒有意義，則此動詞應是不及物動詞。

例如：我 Love 你，你被我 Love

　　　我愛你，你被我愛。句子意思清楚，Love 應是及物動詞。

又如：我 Arrive 你，你被我 Arrive

　　　我到達你，你被我到達。語意不通，因此可知 Arrive 是不及物動詞。

此公式中的「我＿＿＿＿你」、「你被我＿＿＿＿」，可換成事物來代替，如下：

我＿＿＿＿事物、事物被我＿＿＿＿

例如：I wrote a letter.（我寫了一封信。）

　　　The letter was written by me.（這封信被我寫了。）

語意通順，可見 Write 是及物動詞。

第二項　動名詞與現在分詞

同樣都是由動詞＋ ing 形成，看起來一樣，但用法卻不同：

■ 動名詞：顧名思義就是可當做名詞用，主要被用於：

1. 作為及物動詞的受詞。

　　例如：I enjoy dancing.（我喜歡跳舞。）

2. 作為介系詞後面的受詞。

　　例如：I look forward to seeing you soon.（我期待很快能見到您。）

3. 作為 Be 動詞的主詞補語。

　　例如：Seeing is <u>believing</u>.（百聞不如一見。）

■ 現在分詞：主要被用於：

1. 表動作正在進行的狀態時，翻譯成「正在……」。

　　例如：He is <u>dancing</u>.（他正在跳舞。）

2. 作為不完全不及物動詞的主詞補語，當形容詞用，翻譯成「……的」。

　　例如： The story is <u>interesting</u>.

○ **補充說明** ○

如何分辨動名詞與現在分詞？

a. 動詞＋ing 可翻譯成（正在……）時，就是現在分詞。

　　例如：He is painting the house.（他正在粉刷房子。）
　　　　　所以 Painting 是現在分詞表動作在進行的狀態。
　　　　　His job is <u>painting</u> houses.（他的工作是粉刷房子。）
　　　　　如翻成他的工作是正在粉刷房子，則語意不通，
　　　　　但翻譯成他的工作是（……的）時，則意思通順，
　　　　　所以此處的 Painting 是動名詞做主詞補語用。

b. Be 動詞之後的「<u>動詞＋ing</u>」可與主詞互換時，語意不變，此「動詞＋ing」就是動名詞，若不能互換（換了以後意思不通）就是現在分詞。

　　例如：He is <u>driving the bus</u>. → <u>Driving the bus</u> is he.，
　　　　　互換後顯然不通，所以 Driving 不是動名詞。
　　　　　但 His job is <u>driving bus</u>. → <u>Driving bus</u> is his job. 可以互換，語意清楚通順，所以此處的 Driving 是動名詞，動名詞因具有名詞的功能，可做補語又可做主詞。

第三項　現在分詞與過去分詞

現在分詞由動詞＋ing 形成，而過去分詞由動詞＋ ed 或其他不規則變化而成，兩者很容易分辨，在做修飾用時含有形容詞的性質，但用法卻有不同。

一 用做形容詞

現在分詞在修飾時，具：(1) 主動的意味、(2) 表進行的概念；而過去分詞則含有 (1) 被動的意味或 (2) 表完成的概念。

1. 置於名詞之前。

   例如：A <u>smiling</u> girl（微笑著的女孩）

   現在分詞 Smiling 修飾 Girl，表進行的概念，正在微笑的或微笑中的。

   又如：A <u>broken</u> pencil（折斷的鉛筆）

   過去分詞 Broken 修飾 Pencil，不能用現在分詞 Breaking 來修飾，因爲鉛筆不會主動正在折斷，而是已經斷了的。

2. 置於名詞之後。

   例如：This is the letter <u>written</u> by Peter.

   （這就是 Peter 寫的信。）

   信是被寫而且已經完成，所以用過去分詞，不可用現在分詞 Writing 來修飾。

   又如：The man <u>writing</u> a letter is Peter.

   （正在寫信的那個男人是 Peter。）

   人當然可以寫信，而且表示正在寫信的狀態，所以用現在分詞。

二 用做主詞補語

現在分詞具有主動的概念，表示「令人……的」意思，而過去分詞具有被動的意味，表示「感到……的」。

1. 置於 Be 動詞之後。

　例如：The story is <u>interesting</u>.

　　（這故事是有趣的。）即令人有興趣的。

　　I am <u>interested</u> in the story.

　　（我對這故事感到有興趣。）

　　The news is <u>exciting</u>.

　　（這消息是令人興奮的。）

　　I am <u>excited</u> to hear the news.

　　（我對這消息感到興奮。）

2. 置於不完全不及物動詞，如連綴動詞之後（Seem、Appear、Become、Turn、Remain 等）。

　例如：He seems <u>tired</u>.

　　（他似乎累了。）即感到疲倦了的意思。

三 用做受詞補語：表示主動、進行的概念用現在分詞，表示被動、已發生的概念用過去分詞。

置於不完全及物動詞，如感官動詞之後（Hear、Find、See、Feel 等）。

　例如：He found the cat <u>killing</u> a fish.

　　（他發現那隻貓正在殺魚。）

He found the fish <u>killed</u>.

（他發現這隻魚被殺死了。）

I heard the door <u>broken</u>.

（我聽到這扇門被打破了。）

 名詞子句與名詞片語

一 相同點：顧名思義兩者都具有名詞的特性，可做主詞、受詞或 Be 動詞之後的補語。

二 不同點：名詞子句是由任何一個以主詞為起首的完整句子，前面冠上 That 或 Whether 所形成。或是由疑問詞（Where、When、How、What 等）所引導的問句變化所形成。

例如：That he likes me is a fact.（他喜歡我是事實。）

　　　名詞子句 That he likes me 當主詞。

又如：I don't know what he bought Yesterday.

　　　（我不知道他昨天買了什麼東西。）

　　　名詞子句 What he bought yesterday 當受詞。

而名詞片語係由「疑問詞＋不定詞片語」所形成，不含主詞和述詞，不像名詞子句有完整的句子結構。

例如：I do not <u>know how to do it</u>.（我不知道如何做此事。）

　　　名詞片語 How to do it 當 Know 的受詞。

又如：<u>Where</u> to go is my problem.（要去哪裡是我的難題。）

　　　名詞片語 Where to go 當主詞。

三 名詞子句有三個種類

1. 由 That 引導的子句。

    例如：It is true <u>that the earth is round</u>.

2. 由 Whether 引導的子句。

    例如：I care <u>whether she loves me</u>.

3. 由疑問詞引導的子句。

    例如：<u>Where he lives</u> is a question.

附錄

4

中國大陸銀行直接開至臺灣的 L/C 實例

```
---------------- Instance Type and Transmission ------------
Original received from SWIFT
Priority             : Normal
Message Output Reference : 1028 030416CCBCTWTPA2127173691811
Correspondent Input Reference : 1028 030416CIBKCNBJA2152820834421
------------------------------ Message Header ---------------
Swift Output      : FIN 700 Issue of a Documentary Credit
Sender            : CIBKCNBJ215
                    CITIC INDUSTRIAL BANK
                    (SUZHOU BRANCH)
                    SUZHOU CN
Receiver          : CCBCTWTP212
                    CHANG HWA COMMERCIAL BANK LTD.
                    (OFFSHORE BANKING BRANCH)
                    TAIPEI TW
------------------------------ Message Text -----------------
  27: Sequence of Total
      1/1
 40A: Form of Documentary Credit
      IRREVOCABLE
  20: Documentary Credit Number
      21501LC0300076
 31C: Date of Issue
      030416
 31D: Date and Place of Expiry
      030531TAIWAN
  50: Applicant
      ████████████████████████.
      LTD.
      █████████████, SUZHOU NEW
      DISTRICT, JIANGSU, CHINA
  59: Beneficiary - Name & Address
      █████████████████████████
      LIMITED
      ███████████████████,TAICHUNG.
      TAIWAN
 32B: Currency Code, Amount
      Currency       : USD (US DOLLAR)
      Amount         :        .#33,480.00#
 41D: Available With...By... - Name&Addr
      ANY BANK IN TAIWAN
      BY NEGOTIATION
 42C: Drafts at...
      AT SIGHT FOR 100 PCT OF INVOICE
      VALUE
 42A: Drawee - BIC
      CIBKCNBJ215
      CITIC INDUSTRIAL BANK
      (SUZHOU BRANCH)
      SUZHOU  CN
 43P: Partial Shipments
      ALLOWED
 43T: Transhipment
      ALLOWED
```

```
16/04/03-10:27:10        OUTEXPD-1240-000001              2
```

√ 44A: On Board/Disp/Taking Charge at/f
ANY TAIWAN PORT
√ 44B: For Transportation to...
SHANGHAI CHINA
　44C: Latest Date of Shipment
030516
　45A: Descriptn of Goods &/or Services
COMMODITY:
ABS RESIN
▉▉▉▉▉▉▉▉▉▉▉▉
QUANTITY:36MTS UNIT PRICE:▉▉▉▉▉▉▉▉▉
TOTAL AMOUNT:USD33,480.00
CIF SHANGHAI
　46A: Documents Required
　1.MANUALLY SIGNED COMMERCIAL INVOICE IN 3 COPIES INDICATING
CONTRACT NO.
　2.FULL SET LESS ONE 2/3 ORIGINAL CLEAN ON BOARD OCEAN BILLS
OF LADING MARKED 'FREIGHT PREPAID' MADE OUT TO ORDER AND
BLANK ENDORSED NOTIFYING APPLICANT WITH ITS FULL NAME
AND ADDRESS.
　3.INSURANCE POLICY/CERTIFICATE IN 2 COPIES FOR 110PCT OF THE
INVOICE VALUE, BLANK ENDORSED, COVERING OCEAN MARINE
TRANSPORTATION ALL RISKS AND WAR RISKS SHOWING CLAIMS
PAYABLE IN CHINA,IN CURRENCY OF THE DRAFT.
　4.PACKING LIST OR WEIGHT MEMO IN 2 COPIES INDICATING QUANTITY OR
GROSS AND NET WEIGHT OF EACH PACKAGE.
　5.CERTIFICATE OF QUANTITY/WEIGHT IN 2 COPIES ISSUED BY
BENEFICIARY.
　6.BENEFICIARY'S CERTIFICATE CONFIRMING THAT ONE SET OF ORIGINAL
DOCUMENT INCLUDING INVOICE,PACKING LIST,1/3 B/L HAVE BEEN
SENT TO THE APPLICANT BY 'DHL' WITHIN TWO DAYS AFTER
SHIPPING DATE.
　7.BENEFICIARY'S CERTIFICATE CONFIRMING THEIR ACCEPTANCE OR
NON-ACCEPTANCE OF THE AMENDMENTS ISSUED UNDER THIS CREDIT
QUOTING THE RELEVANT AMENDMENT NUMBER, SUCH CERTIFICATE IS
NOT REQUIRED IF NO AMENDMENT HAS BEEN ISSUED UNDER THIS CREDIT.
　47A: Additional Conditions
　1.THE CREDIT IS ISSUED SUBJECT TO THE UNIFORM CUSTOMS AND
PRACTICE FOR DOCUMENTARY CREDIT (1993 REVISIOIN) ICC -
PUBLICATION NO.500.
　2.DOCUMENTS ISSUED EARLIER THAN L/C ISSUING DATE NOT ACCEPTABLE.
　3.T/T REIMBURSEMENTS ARE NOT ALLOWED.
　4.AN EXTRA COPIES OF DOCUMENTS ARE REQUESTED TO BE PRESENTED FOR
ISSUING BANK'S FILE ONLY.
　5.ALL DOCUMENTS SHOULD BE ISSUED IN ENGLISH AND BEAR OUR L/C NO.
　6.ALL PRESENTATIONS CONTAINING DISCREPANCY(IES) WILL ATTRACT A
DISCREPANCY FEE OF USD50.00 OR EQUIVALENT PULS TELEX AND
HOLDING CHARGES, IF ANY. THIS CHARGE WILL BE LEVIED WHETHER
OR NOT WE ELECT TO CONSULT THE APPLICANT FOR A WAIVER IN
ACCORDANCE WITH UCP500 ARTICLE 14. THESE CHARGES WILL ALWAYS
BE FOR THE ACCOUNT OF THE BENEFICIARY.
　7.DRAFTS DRAWN HEREUNDER MUST BEAR OUR NAME THE CREDIT NO. AND
DATE.
　8.NOTWITHSTANDING THE PROVISIONS OF UCP500 WE GIVE THE
NOTICE OF REFUSAL OF DOCUMENTS PRESENTED DER THIS CREDIT.

附錄

5

臺灣直接開至中國大陸銀行的 L/C 實例

```
------------------------ Instance Type and Transmission ----------
Notification (Transmission) of Original sent to SWIFT (ACK)
Network Delivery Status  : Network Ack
Priority/Delivery        : Normal
Message Input Reference  : 1755 030416CCBCTWTPAXXX7175124179
-------------------------- Message Header --------------------------
      Swift Input   : FIN 700 Issue of a Documentary Credit
✓  Sender        : CCBCTWTPXXX
                     CHANG HWA COMMERCIAL BANK LTD.
                     TAIPEI TW
✓  Receiver      : BKCHCNBJ85B
                     BANK OF CHINA
                     (JILIN CITY BRANCH)
                     JILIN CN
-------------------------- Message Text --------------------------
   27: Sequence of Total
       1/4
   40A: Form of Documentary Credit
        IRREVOCABLE
   20: Documentary Credit Number
       3AQQH20    -5210
   31C: Date of Issue
        030416
✓  31D: Date and Place of Expiry
        030619 IN THE BENEFICIARY'S COUNTRY
✓   50: Applicant
         (台灣開狀人名稱及地址)

✓   59: Beneficiary - Name & Address
         (大陸受益人名稱及地址)


   32B: Currency Code, Amount
        Currency       : USD (US DOLLAR)
        Amount         :         #229,800.00#
   41D: Available With...By... - Name&Addr
        AVAILABLE WITH ANY BANK
        BY NEGOTIATION
   42C: Drafts at...
        DRAFTS AT SIGHT
   42A: Drawee - BIC
        CCBCTWTP
        CHANG HWA COMMERCIAL BANK LTD.
        TAIPEI  TW
   43P: Partial Shipments
        PERMITTED
   43T: Transhipment
        PERMITTED
✓  44A: On Board/Disp/Taking Charge at/f
        DALIAN
✓  44B: For Transportation to...
        KEELUNG VIA ISHIGAKI JAPAN
   44C: Latest Date of Shipment
        030605
   71B: Charges
        +ALL BANKING CHARGES OUTSIDE TAIWAN
        AND REIMBURSEMENT CHARGE ARE FOR
```

```
            BENEFICIARY'S ACCOUNT.
    48: Period for Presentation
         DOCUMENTS HAVE TO BE PRESENTED
         WITHIN 14 DAYS AFTER DATE OF
  16/04/03-17:54:25              IN2-8110-000013

         SHIPMENT BUT NOT LATER THAN L/C
         EXPIRY DATE.
    49: Confirmation Instructions
         WITHOUT
    78: Instr to Payg/Accptg/Negotg Bank
         +TO THE NEGOTIATING BANK ONLY: PLEASE DEDUCT ALL CHARGES LIAB
         TO ADVISING BANK, AND WHEN DOCUMENTS PRESENTED WITH DISCREPAN
         PLEASE ALSO DEDUCT USD50.00 (OR EQUIVALENT) FROM PROCEEDS UPO
         PAYMENT.
         +THE NEGOTIATING BANK MUST SEND THE REQUIRED DOCUMENTS DIRECT
         US (P.O. BOX 672, NO. 57 CHUNG SHAN NORTH ROAD, SEC. 2, TAIPE
         10419 TAIWAN, REPUBLIC OF CHINA) IN ONE SET BY COURIER.
         +TO THE NEGOTIATING BANK ONLY:
         IF RECEIVING THE SHIPPING DOCUMENTS IN COMPLIANCE WITH THE
         TERMS AND CONDITIONS, WE SHALL EFFECT THE PAYMENT (DEDUCT OUR
         OPERATING CHARGES) AS PER YOUR INSTRUCTIONS.
    72: Sender to Receiver Information
         THIS CREDIT IS SUBJECT TO UCP 1993
         (ICC 500).
----------------------------- Message Trailer -----------------------------
   (MAC:46A428F9)
   (CHK:F77CC32831E4)
----------------------------- Interventions -----------------------------
   Category      : Network Report
   Creation Time : 16/04/03 17:53:22
   Application   : SWIFT Interface
   Operator      : SYSTEM
   Text
   (1:F21CCBCTWTPAXXX7175324178)(4:(177:0304161755)(451:0))
```

附錄

6

中國大陸對貿易術語（交易條件）的詮釋（註：2010 年版國貿條規）

E 組	EXW	EX WORKS	工厂交货
F 組	FCA	Free Carrier	货交承运人
	FAS	Free Alongside Ship	船边交货
	FOB	Free on Board	装运港船上交货
C 組	CFR	Cost and Freight	成本加运费
	CIF	Cost, Insurance and Freight	成本加保险费、运费
	CPT	Carriage Paid To	运费付至
	CIP	Carriage and Insurance Paid To	运费、保险费付至
D 組	DAF	Delivered At Frontier	边境交货
	DES	Delivered Ex Ship	目的港船上交货
	DEQ	Delivered Ex Quay	目的港码头交货
	DDU	Delivered Duty Unpaid	未完税交货
	DDP	Delivered Duty Paid	完税后交货

貿易术语的诠释

- ### 工厂交货（……指定地）：EXW（...named place）

  EXW 術語是賣方在其所在地（即工廠、工場、倉庫等）將貨物交付買方時，即履行了交貨義務，除非另有約定，賣方不承擔將貨物裝上買方備妥的運輸車輛或辦理出口清關手續的責任。這是賣方承擔責任最小的一種貿易術語。買方則承擔自賣方所在地將貨物運至所需目的地的一切費用及風險。

- ### 货交承运人（……指定地）：FCA（...named place）

  FCA 術語是指賣方在指定地將經出口清關的貨物交付買方指定的承運人監管時，即履行了交貨義務。如買方未指明確切的地點，賣方可在規定的交貨地或地段內，選擇在何處由承運人接管貨物。按商業慣例，在與承運人訂立合同時（如鐵路或航空運輸），若需賣方提供協助，賣方可在由買方承擔費用和風險的情況下行事。FCA 術語適用於各種運輸方式，包括多式聯運。

- ### 船边交货（……指定装运港）：FAS（...named port of shipment）

  FAS 術語是指賣方將貨物交到指定的裝運港船邊，即履行了交貨義務。買方自此時起承擔一切費用和貨物滅失或損壞的風險。但如港口吃水淺，船舶不能靠岸，則貨物從碼頭駁運至船邊的一切費用和風險，仍應由賣方承擔。FAS 術語要求買方辦理出口清關手續，適用於海運和內河航運。

- 装运港船上交货（……指定装运港）：FOB（...named port of shipment）

  FOB 術語是指賣方在指定的裝運港，將貨物裝到買方指定的船上，當貨物越過船舷後，賣方即履行了交貨義務。買方自該交貨點起，承擔一切費用和貨物滅失或損壞的風險。FOB 術語要求賣方辦理出口清關手續，適用於海運和內河航運。

- 成本加运费（……指定目的港）：CFR（...named port of destination）

  CFR 術語是指賣方必須負擔貨物運至指定目的港所需的成本和運費。當貨物在裝運港越過船舷後、買方承擔貨物滅失或損壞的風險，以及由於貨物已裝上船後發生的裝船通知，以至買方無法辦理保險或漏運險，賣方應承擔貨物在運輸途中的風險損失。CFR 術語要求賣方辦理出口清關手續，適用於海運和內河航運。

- 成本加保险费、运费（……指定目的港）：CIF（...named port of destination）

  CIF 術語是指賣方必須負擔貨物運至指定目的港所需的成本和運費，並為貨物的運輸途中滅失或損壞的買方風險辦理貨運險和支付保險費。當貨物在裝運港越過船舷後，買方承擔貨物滅失或損壞的一切風險。CIF 屬於要求賣方辦理出口清關手續，適用於海運和內河航運。

- 运费付至（……指定目的地）：CPT（...named place of destination)

CPT 術語是指賣方支付貨物運至指定目的地的運費。買方承擔貨物交由第一承運人接管時起，產生的一切額外費用和貨物在運輸途中滅失或損壞的風險。CPT 術語要求賣方辦理出口清關手續，適用於各種運輸方式，包括多式聯運。

- 运费、保险费付至（……指定目的地）：CIP（...named place of destination）

CIP 術語是指賣方必須負擔貨物運至指定目的地的運費，並爲貨物在運輸途中滅失或損壞的買方風險辦理貨運險和支付保險費。買方承擔貨物交由第一承運人接管時起產生的一切額外費用和貨物在運輸途中滅失或損壞的風險。CIP 術語要求賣方辦理出口清關手續，適用於各種運輸方式，包括多式聯運

- 边境交货（……指定地）：DAF（...named place）

DAF 術語是指賣方在邊境指定地和地點，將經出口清關的貨物交付買方處置後，即履行了交貨義務。買方承擔交貨後發生的一切費用和風險。DAF 術語主要用於鐵路或公路貨物運輸，也適用於其他各種運輸方式。

- 目的港船上交货（……指定目的港）：DES（...named port of destination）

DES 術語是指賣方將貨物運至指定的目的港，並在船上將未

經清關的貨物交付買方後，即履行了交貨義務。買方承擔船上貨物交由其處置後發生的一切費用和風險，DES 術語適用於海運和內河航運。

- 目的港码头交货（关税已付）（……指定目的港）：
  DEQ（Duty paid）（...named port of destination）

  DEQ（Duty paid）術語是指賣方將貨物運至指定的目的港碼頭，將經過清關的貨物交付買方後，即履行了交貨義務。賣方承擔將貨物運至指定目的港碼頭的一切費用和風險，包括關稅、稅捐及因交貨而發生的費用：買方承擔貨物交由其處置後發生的一切費用和風險。如雙方要求買方辦理貨物進口清關手續並支付關稅，應使用「關稅未付」一詞。DEQ 術語適用於海運和內河航運。

- 未完税交货（……指定目的地）：DDU（...named place of destination）

- 完税后交货（……指定目的地）：DDP（...named place of destination）

  DDP 術語是指賣方將貨物運至進口國的指定目的地，即履行了交貨義務。這是買方承擔責任最小的一種貿易術語。賣方承擔將貨物運至指定目的地的一切費用和風險。包括關稅、稅捐及有關交貨的其他費用，並辦理貨物進口清關手續。DDP 術語適用於各種運輸方式。
  DDU 術語在新的國貿條規已無收錄，本書僅列示，不再說明。

在貨物進（出）口中常用的價格術語，主要是 FOB、CFR、CIF。

三種常用的價格術語都是裝運港交貨，買賣雙方的風險劃分都是以貨物裝上船為其界線，但主要區別是雙方辦理的手續和支付費用不同，其主要異同如下表：

價格術語	風 險	手 續		費 用	
	誰承擔裝上船後的風險	誰辦理租船訂艙	誰辦理保險	誰支付到目的港運費	誰支付保險費
FOB	買方	買方	買方	買方	買方
CFR	買方	賣方	買方	賣方	買方
CIF	買方	賣方	賣方	賣方	賣方

附錄

7 中國大陸報關常用英文術語

英文	中文
Above 〜 stated	上述的
Acquisition of technology	技术引进
Acceptance	承兑
Ad. val.（Ad valorem）	从价
Ad valorem duties	从价税
Ad valorem tax	从价税
Air transport	航空运输
Airway bill	空运单
Anticipatory L/C	预支信用证
A. R. — All Risks	一切险
Back to back L/C	背对背信用证
Baggage Declaration for incoming passengers	入境旅客行李物品申报单
Barter	易货贸易
Bill of Exchange, Draft	汇票
B/L — bill of lading	提单
Bonded warehouse	保税仓库
Bulky goods	大宗货

英文	中文
Cash payment	现金付款
CFR — Cost and Freight	成本加运费
CIF — Cost, Insurance and Freight	成本加保费、运费
CIP — Carriage and Insurance Paid to	运费、保险费付至目的地
CIC — China Insurance Clause	中国人民保险公司海洋运输货物保险条款
Claims and complaints	索赔
Clean on board B/L	清洁、已装船提单
Collection	托收
Compensation	补偿、赔偿
Compensation trade	补偿贸易
Confirmed L/C	保兑信用证
CPT — Carriage Paid to	运费付至目的地
D/A — Documents against Acceptance	承兑交单
DAF — Delivered at Frontier	边境交货
D/D — Demand Draft	票汇
DDP — Delivered and Duty Paid	目的地交货关税已付
DDU — Delivered and Duty Unpaid	目的地交货关税未付
Declaration for Export Cargo	出口货物报关单
DES — Delivered Ex Ship	目的港船上交货

英文	中文
DEQ — Delivered Ex Quay	目的港码头交货关税已付
Direct B/L	直达提单
Documentary L/C	跟单信用证
Documents against Payment after sight (D/P after Sight)	远期付款交单
Documents against Payment at sight (D/P Sight)	即期付款交单
Domestic value	国内价格
D/P — Documents against Payment	付款交单
D/P Sight	即期付款交单
D/P after Sight	远期付款交单
D/P T/R	付款交单凭信托收据借贷
Dumping	倾销
Duty ～ pay value	完税价格
Endorsement	背书
Exclusive right	独家经营权
Export license	出口许可证
Export subsidy	出口补贴
Ex work	工厂交货
FAS — Free Alongside ship	船边交货
FCA — Free Carrier	货交承运人、多式联运
FOB — Free on Board	装运港船上交货
FOBT — FOB Trimmed	船上交货并平舱

英文	中文
FPA — Free from Particular Average	平安险
Free port	自由港
Free trade zone	自由贸易区
Green Channel	绿色通道（即：免税通道）
IBRD — International Bank for Reconstruction and Development	国际复兴开发银行
I.C.C — Institute Cargo Clause	英国协会条款
IDA — International Development Association	国际开发协会
IFC — International Finance Corporation	国际金融公司
IMF — International Monetary Fund	国际货币基金组织
Importer	进口商
Individual's article	个人物品
Inspection certificate of health	产地检验证书
Inspection certificate of quality	品质检验证书
Inspection certificate on damaged cargo	残损检验证书
Installment	分期付款
Insurance policy	保险单
In duplicate	一式二份
In triplicate	一式三份

英文	中文
In quadruplicate	一式四份
In quintuplicate	一式五份
In bulk	大批（散裝）
Irrevocable L/C	不可撤消信用证
Late payment fee	滞纳金
L/C — Letter of Credit	信用证
Limited company	有限公司
Line of business	经营范围
Means of transport	运输方式
Memorandum	备忘录
Non ～ tariff	非关税壁垒
More or less allowed	允许溢短裝
M/T — Mail Transfer	信汇
Nude cargo	裸装货
On board	已装船
Open B/L、Order B/L	不记名提单、指示提单
Outer packing	外包装
Pack	包装
Package (pkg)	件
Packed in bags	袋装
Packed in cases	箱装
Packed in drums	桶装
Packing mark	包装标志

英文	中文
Passengers' Baggage and Personal Postal Parcels	中华人民共和国关于入境旅客行李物品和个人邮递物品征收进口税办法
Payment agreement	付款协议
Payment in advance	预付协议
Port director	口岸海关关长
Port of embarkation	装运港
Port of loading	装运港
Port of shipment	装运港
Port of unloading	卸货港
Port surcharge	港口附加费
Practice	习惯做法
Premium	保险费
Processing on given materials	来料加工
Quality	质量
Quantity discount	数量折扣
Rate of freight	运费率
Remittance	汇付
Reciprocal L/C	对开信用证
Red Channel (i.e. passage for passengers carrying dutiable articles)	红色通道（即：应税通道）
Registered	已登记的
Revocable L/C	可撤消信用证

英文	中文
Revolving L/C	循环信用证
Rules for the Interpretation of the Nomenclature	税则目录归类总规则
Rules for Customs Supervision and Control over Inward and Outbound Passenger's Baggage	海关对进出境旅客行李物品监管办法
Rules for Customs Supervision and Control over Passenger's Luggage	海关对旅客行李物品监督管理的规定
Rules of origin	原产地规则
SDR — Special Drawing Rights	特别提款权
Sealing marks	封志
Seasonal duty	季节性关税
Section chief	科长
Security	保证金
Shipped bill	已装船提单
Short or non ～ levying of duties	少征或漏征
Short shipment	短装
Sight L/C	即期信用证
Smuggled goods	走私货物
Smuggled article	走私物品
Smuggling activities	走私活动
Sole agent	独家代理人

英文	中文
Special Customs ～ privileged facilities	海关提供的特殊优惠措施
Specific tariff	从量税
Statistic units	统计单位
Submit the relevant papers and certificates to the customs	向海关递交有关单证
Subsidiary company	子公司
Supervision and control over goods	对货物的监管
Submit an application for reconsideration of the case	提出案件再审的申请
Table of rates	税率表
Take delivery of goods	提货
Tariff barrier	关税壁垒
Tariff classification	税则分类
Tariff commission	税则委员会
Tariff committee	关税委员会
Tariff concession	关税减让
Tariff quotas	关税配额
Temporarily imported (exported) goods	暂时进（出）口货物
Temporarily duty ～ free	暂免关税
The above ～ mentioned goods	上述货物

英文	中文
Through goods	通运货物
Transferable L/C	可转让信用证
Trust Receipt	信托收据
T/T — Telegraphic Transfer	电汇
Usance L/C	远期信用证
World Trade Organization (WTO)	世界贸易组织
WPA — With Average or With Particular Average	水渍险
W/W — Warehouse to Warehouse	仓至仓条款

附錄

8　中國大陸船務常用英文術語

一　英文說明及中國大陸譯文

1

Freight Forwarding Agency:

A commercial agency that makes all the arrangements for the shipment of freight by either air or surface means. In the freight business it performs services somewhat similar to those performed by a travel agency for passengers.

翻譯

货运代理公司：

安排所有空中或地面运输的商业性代理公司。在运输业务中，起着类似客运旅行社对旅客所起的作用。

2

Air Waybill:

A list of goods together with shipping instructions for each shipment of air freight. The air waybill is numbered, and normally the number appears on each piece in the shipment. The form in common use is one that has been approved by IATA. The air waybill might be called the 'ticket' for air freight. The abbreviation AWB is often used for the air waybill.

翻譯

航空货运单：

指附有每批航空货运说明的货运清单，航空货运单编有号码，而且通常都要出现在该批货物中的每一件货物上，所使用的表格是由国际航空运输协会批准的。可以把货运单看做航空货运的「客票」。航空货运单常缩写为 ABW。

3

Customs Broker:

An agent who handles customs and other government formalities on freight shipment .

翻譯

海关代理：

指经办货运的海关及其他政府手续的代理。

4

Consign:

To turn something over for shipment. The goods consigned are called a consignment; the person or firm that consigns is the consignor; the person or firm that is going to receive the shipment is the consignee. The last term is the one most commonly in use.

🎯 **翻譯**

委托：

即將某物委托他人运输。所委托的货物叫做委托物；委托的人或公司是受托人。受托人是最常用的术语。

5

Master and House Air Waybills:

The freight forwarder may consolidate the consignments of several independent shippers that are intended for the same airport of destination and dispatch them together under one air waybill (AWB) issued by the carrier, known as master air waybill (MAWB), with a cargo manifest detailing such consignments attached to the MAWB. The freight forwarder in turn issues to each shipper its own AWB, known as a house air waybill (HAWB).

翻譯

主货单和分货单：

　　货运代理将几位货主托运的货物合并在一起托运到同一个目的地机场，并把所有的货物填在一张共同的货运单上，这就称为主货单；代理人随后再依次把每件单独的货物填在自配的货运单上，被称为分货单。

6

Shipping Documents:

　　Documents other than transportation receipts or transportation contracts, required to enable shipment to be forwarded or received.

翻譯

货运文件：

　　除了运输收据或运输合同之外，能够作为运输和提取货物凭证的文件。

7

Consolidated Airfreight:

　　Individual shipments combined as one consignment covered by a Master Air Waybill.

◎ **翻譯**

集运货物：

　　填写在主货单上的合并装运（集运）货物。

8

Manifest:

　　Official list of cargo onboard a flight.

◎ **翻譯**

舱单：

　　正式的机载货物清单。

二　英文名詞解釋

1. General Concept of Marine Bills of Lading

　　我国《海商法》第 71 条对提单的陈述为：「提单，是指用以证明海上货物运输合同和货物已经由承运人接收或者装船，以及承运人保证据以交付货物的单证。提单中载明的向记名人交付货物，或者按照指示人的指示交付货物，或者向提单持有人交付货物的条款，构成承运人据以交付货物的保证。」

2. Order bills made out to consignee "or order" can be transferred by them by endorsement.

指示提單上「收貨人」（Consignee）一欄內載明「由某人
指示」（Order of...）可為「托運人指示」、「銀行指示」
和「收貨人指示」等幾種形式。指示提單可流通，採用背書
（Endorsement）形式即可轉讓。

3. Endorsement 背書

背書是由提單轉讓人在提單的背面寫明受讓人並簽字的一種
手續。記名背書（special endorsement）是背書人在提單背
面寫明被背書人的背書，表明承運人應將貨物交給被背書
人或按其進一步的指示交貨。不記名背書（endorsement in
blank）是指背書人在提單背面不寫明被背書人，而只簽署自
己姓名的背書，此時，承運人應將貨物交給出示提單的人。

4. Direct bills of lading and through bills of lading

根據貨物的運輸方式，提單可分為直達提單、海上聯運提單
和多式聯運提單。直達提單（Direct B/L）是指貨物從裝貨
港受載後，中途不經換船，直接運至目的港卸船交付貨物的
提單。海上聯運提單（Ocean through B/L）是指貨物從裝貨
港裝船後，在中途卸船，交給其他承運人用其他船舶接運
至目的港的提單。多式聯運提單（Combined transport B/L,
Multimodal transport B/L, intermodal transport B/L）多用於國
際集裝箱運輸（因此，有時稱為 Container bills of lading），

指承运人将货物以包括海上运输在内的两种或多种运输方式，从一地运至另一地的提单。

5. Clean versus foul bills of lading

根据提单上有无不良批注（Remarks），提单可分为清洁提单和不清洁提单。清洁提单是提单上没有任何关于货物外表状态不良批注的提单，表明承运人在接受货物时，货物的外表状态良好（In apparent good order and condition）。贸易合同和信用证（Letter of credit）一般都规定卖方必须凭清洁提单向银行结汇。不清洁提单上为有关于货物外表状态的不良批注。银行在办理结汇时一般不接受这种不清洁提单。

三 船務常用術語

英文	中文
Marine insurance	海上保险
Notice of claim	索赔通知
Partial loss	部分损失
Perils of the sea	海上风险
Rate of premium	保险费率
Recovery	追偿
Returns of premium	保险退费
Validity of policy	保险单的有效期
Valued policy	定值保险单
Voyage policy	航次保险单
War risk	战争险
Wear and tear	自然磨损
Insurance fund	保险基金
Insurance company	保险公司
Insurance contract	保险合同
Insurance clauses	保险条款
Insurance period	保险期限
Insurance agent	保险代理人
Abandonment	委付
Actual total loss	实际全损
Constructive total loss	推定全损
Force majeure	不可抗力
Franchise	相对免赔額

英文	中文
Full insurance	足额保险
General average contribution	共同海损分摊
Insurance broker	保险经纪人
In transit	运输中
Particular average	单独海损
General average	共同海损
Partial loss	部分损失
Stranded vessel	搁浅船
Free of Particular Average (FPA)	平安险（单独海损不赔）
With Average / With Particular Average (WA/WPA)	水渍险
All Risks (AR)	一切险
War and Strikes, Riots and Civil Commotions	战争、罢工、暴动和民变（风险）
Bulk cargo	散货
Deductible franchise	绝对免赔额
General cargo	杂货
Inherent vice	内在缺陷、固有缺陷

四　國貿條規交貨條件專用術語

英文	中文
CFR (Cost and Freight)	成本加运费（……指定目的港）
FOB (Free on Board)	船上交货（……指定装运港）
CIF (Cost, Insurance and Freight)	成本、保险费加运费（……指定目的港）
FCA (Free Carrier)	货交承运人（……指定地点）
CPT (Carriage Paid to)	运费付至（……指定目的地）
CIP (Carriage and Insurance Paid to)	运费、保险费付至（……指定目的地）
Inland waterway transport	内河运输
Clear the goods for export	办理货物出口清关手续
Insurance policy	保险单
Insurance premium	保险费
Ocean freight	海运运费
Freight rate	运费率、运价
Transhipment additional	转船附加费
Port additional	港口附加费
Port congestion surcharge	港口拥挤附加费
Alteration of destination additional	变更卸货港附加费
Deviation surcharge	绕航附加费
Optional additional	选卸附加费

英文	中文
Bunker surcharge	燃油附加费
Additional for excess of liability	超额责任附加费
Demurrage	滞期费
Dispatch money	速遣费
Shipping space	舱位
Ocean freight rate	海运运费
Tramp rate	不定期船运费率
Liner freight rate	班轮运费率
Liner operator	班轮营运人
Stowage factor	积载因数
Break bulk cargo	件杂货
Adjustment factors	调整因素
Currency adjustment factor (CAF)	货币贬值调整因素、货币贬值附加费
Bunker adjustment factor (BAF)	燃油价格调整因素、燃油附加费
Stale bill of lading	过期提单
Short form bill of lading	简式提单
Long form bill of lading	长式提单
Combined transport bill of lading or multimodal transport bill of lading	多式联运提单
Intermodal transport bill of lading (American English)	多式联运提单

英文	中文
On deck bill of lading	舱面货提单
Minimum freight bill of lading	最低运费提单
Deviation	绕航
Delay in delivery	延迟交货
Limitation of liability	责任限制
Receiver	受货人
Holder of bill of lading	提单持有人
Sailing schedule	船期表
Endorsement of bill of lading	提单背书
Endorsement in blank	空白背书
Transfer of bill of lading	提单转让
Hague Rules	《海牙规则》
Hague-Visby Rules	《海牙—维斯比规则》
Hamburg rules	《汉堡规则》
Carriage of Goods by Sea Act (COGSA)	海上货物运输法
Arrival notice	到货通知、到港通知
Notify party	通知方
As per	按照
Delivery order	提货单
Full set	全套
Bank draft	银行汇票
Documentary credit	跟单信用证
Issuing bank	开证行

英文	中文
Negotiating bank	押汇银行
Freight manifest	运费清单
Shipping order	装货单
Loading list or cargo list	装货清单
Dangerous cargo list	危险品清单
Damage cargo list	货物残损单
Cargo tracer	货物查询单
Actual carrier	实际承运人
Voyage charter	航次租船
Bareboat charter	光船租赁
Cancelling date	解约日
Laytime	装卸期限
Multimodal transportation	多式联运
Stowage plan	积载图
Handling	搬运
Dunnage	衬垫
Lashing	绑扎
Segregation or separation	隔票
Notice of readiness	准备就绪通知书
Demurrage	滞期
Despatch	速遣
Liner service	班轮运输
Sailing schedule	船期表

英文	中文
Seaworthiness	适航
Cargo worthiness	适货
Shipowner	船舶所有人、船东
Ship operator	船舶经营人
Merchant ship	商船
Passenger ship	客船
General cargo ship	杂货船
Oil tanker	油船
Container ship	集装箱船
Multipurpose cargo vessel	多用途货船
Roll on/ roll off ship or ro/ro ship	滚装船
Customs clearance	结关（证书）
Entry Inwards	进口报关单
Import Manifest	进口载货清单、进口舱单
Load line	载重线
Safety radio telegraphy	无线电报安全
Safety equipment	设备安全
Certificate of registry	登记证书
Crew list	船员名单
Stores list	物料清单
Entry Outwards	出口报关单
Port clearance	结关
Export Manifest	出口载货清单、出口舱单
Bill of Entry	报关单

英文	中文
Customs Declaration	报关、海关申报
Inward Permit	进口许可证
Policy of insurance	保险单
Shipping Bill	出口货物明细单、装船通知单
Export Declaration	出口申报单
Customs area	关税领域
Customs broker	报关行
Customs drawback	海关退税
Customs examination	海关检查
Customs formalities	海关手续
Customs frontier	关境
Customs invoice	海关发票
Customs permit	海关许可证
Customs tariff	关税税则
Customs union	关税同盟
Customs warehouse	保税仓库
Goods (held) in bond	保税货物
Bonded warehouse	保税仓库
International trade	国际贸易
Carriage of goods by sea	海上货物运输
Pattern of international trade	国际贸易方式
Shipping market	航运市场
Non-conference lines	非班轮公会航线

英文	中文
Non-vessel operating common carriers (NVOCC)	无营运船公共承运人
Tramp service	不定期船运输
Conference lines	班轮公会航线
Scheduled service	定期航运
Common carrier	公共承运人
Shipping conference	班轮公会
Freight rate	运费率
Supply and demand	供求
Bill of lading or B/L	提单
Sea waybill	海运单
Shipping note	托运单、装货通知单
Delivery order	提货单
Mate's receipts	大副收据、收货单
Contract of carriage	货物运输合同
Receipt for goods	货物收据
Document of title	物权凭证
Port authorities	港务局、港口主管机关
Shipping space	舱位
Liner transport	班轮运输
Shipping by chartering	租船运输
Sailing schedule	船期表
Liner freight tariff	班轮运价表

英文	中文
Weight ton	重量吨
Measurement ton	尺码吨
Direct additional	直航附加费
Special cargoes	特殊货物
Project cargoes	工程货物
Heavy crane	重吊
Customs terminal	海关站
Trade terms	贸易条款
Trade contract	贸易合同
General cargo	杂货
Transit operations	运输过程
Marine bills of lading	海运提单
International sales of goods	国际货物销售
On board	在船上
Contract of affreightment	货物运输合同
Ship's name	船名
Port of loading	装货港
Contract of carriage	货物运输合同
Order bills of lading	指示提单
Negotiable document	可转让单据
Straight bills of lading	记名提单
Shipped bills of lading	已装船提单
Received for shipment bills of lading	收货待运提单

英文	中文
Direct bills of lading	直达提单
Through bills of lading	联运提单
Shipping company	海运公司、船务公司
Clean bill of lading	清洁提单
Foul bill of lading	不清洁提单
Short shipment	短装、装货不足
Insufficient packing	包装不良、包装不固
Foul bill of lading	不清洁提單
Blank bill of lading	不记名提单
Direct bill of lading	直达提单
Transhipment bill of lading	转船提单
Through bill of lading	联运提单
Long form bill of lading	全式提单
Short form bill of lading	略式提单
Electronic bill of lading	电子提单
Electronic Data Interchange (EDI)	电子数据交换
Letter of indemnity	保函
Due diligence	谨慎处理、恪尽职责
Time bar or time limitation	时效
Seaworthiness	适航
Cargo worthiness	适货
Cargo's apparent order and condition	货物外表状态

英文	中文
Number of B/L	提单签发的份数
Original B/L	正本提单
Copy	副本
UCP600	2007 年修订的国际商会 600 号出版物《跟单信用证统一惯例》
Seaway bill	海运单
Paramount clause	首要条款
Himalaya clause	喜玛拉雅条款
Unknown clause	不知条款
Period of responsibility of carrier	承运人责任期间
Exception clause or exemption clause	除外条款（免责条款）
Jurisdiction clause	管辖权条款
Refrigerated cargo clause	冷藏货条款
Bulk cargo clause	散装货条款
Transhipment clause	转船条款
Timber clause	木材条款

○— 補充說明 —○

ICC 国际商会，全称为 International Chamber of Commerce，1920 年在巴黎成立，其宗旨是促进各国政府采取措施为国际贸易的发展创造条件，加强商业界往来和了解。中国已成为国际商会正式成员国之一。

五　城市中、英文名稱

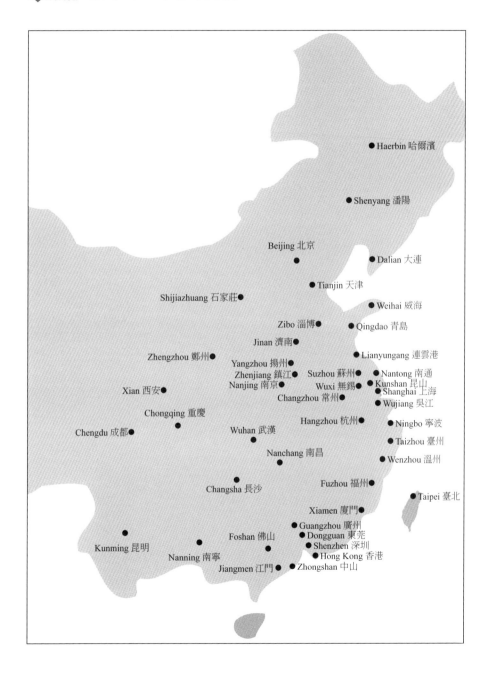

國家圖書館出版品預行編目(CIP)資料

國貿船務英文／許坤金著.--初版.--臺北市：
五南圖書出版股份有限公司, 2023.01
面 ；　公分

ISBN 978-626-343-667-1(平裝)

1.CST: 英語 2.CST: 航務 3.CST: 讀本

805.18　　　　　　　111021343

1069

國貿船務英文

作　　　者 — 許坤金

發 行 人 — 楊榮川

總 經 理 — 楊士清

總 編 輯 — 楊秀麗

副總編輯 — 侯家嵐

責任編輯 — 吳瑀芳

文字校對 — 陳俐君

封面設計 — 王麗娟

出 版 者 — 五南圖書出版股份有限公司

地　　　址：106臺北市大安區和平東路二段339號4樓

電　　　話：(02)2705-5066　　傳　　　真：(02)2706-6100

網　　　址：https://www.wunan.com.tw

電子郵件：wunan@wunan.com.tw

劃撥帳號：01068953

戶　　　名：五南圖書出版股份有限公司

法律顧問：林勝安律師

出版日期：2023年 1 月初版一刷

定　　　價：新臺幣320元

經典永恆・名著常在

五十週年的獻禮——經典名著文庫

五南，五十年了，半個世紀，人生旅程的一大半，走過來了。

思索著，邁向百年的未來歷程，能為知識界、文化學術界作些什麼？

在速食文化的生態下，有什麼值得讓人雋永品味的？

歷代經典・當今名著，經過時間的洗禮，千錘百鍊，流傳至今，光芒耀人；

不僅使我們能領悟前人的智慧，同時也增深加廣我們思考的深度與視野。

我們決心投入巨資，有計畫的系統梳選，成立「經典名著文庫」，

希望收入古今中外思想性的、充滿睿智與獨見的經典、名著。

這是一項理想性的、永續性的巨大出版工程。

不在意讀者的眾寡，只考慮它的學術價值，力求完整展現先哲思想的軌跡；

為知識界開啟一片智慧之窗，營造一座百花綻放的世界文明公園，

任君遨遊、取菁吸蜜、嘉惠學子！